"My Boyfriend Wouldn't Do That!"

"I felt Jason's hands," Emma continued in a shaky voice. "And then he—he pushed me down the stairs!"

"No!" Sydney rose from the bed. "That's *crazy!*"

"Is it?" Emma sat up straighter. "Let me ask you something, Sydney. Did you tell Jason about the money we found?"

"Emma—what does that have to do with anything?" Sydney cried.

"Just answer," Emma demanded. "Did you tell him about the bag of money?"

Sydney's face flushed with guilt. "Yes! Okay, I told him! I told him everything. I'm sorry. I know I promised not to. But Emma, you're wrong about him pushing you down the stairs. He wouldn't do something like that! Why would he?"

"Are you kidding?" Emma asked sarcastically. "For the money!"

R.L. STINE

FEAR STREET®

THE RICH GIRL

Simon Pulse
New York   London   Toronto   Sydney

A Parachute Press book

SIMON PULSE
An imprint of Simon & Schuster Children's Publishing Division
1230 Avenue of the Americas, New York, NY 10020
Copyright © 1997 by Parachute Press, L.L.C.
All rights reserved, including the right of reproduction in whole or in part in any form.
SIMON PULSE and colophon are registered trademarks of
Simon & Schuster, Inc.
FEAR STREET is a registered trademark of Parachute Press, Inc.
Designed by Sammy Yuen Jr.
The text of this book was set in Times.
Manufactured in the United States of America
First Simon Pulse edition June 2005
10 9 8 7 6 5 4 3
Library of Congress Control Number 2004112721
ISBN 1-4169-0324-0

THE RICH GIRL

chapter
1

Sydney Shue tossed the metal scoop back into the popcorn maker and hurried to the other end of the concession counter. "Did you notice who Cathy Harper just walked into the movies with?" she whispered to her best friend, Emma Naylor. "Marty Griffin!"

"You're kidding!" Emma stopped wiping the glass-topped counter and stared in surprise. "I thought they broke up!"

"They did," Sydney replied. "But I just saw them laughing and holding hands and everything. They're obviously back together."

"That's their fourth breakup and make-up this year," Emma remarked. She began wiping the counter again. "Let's see—this is April, right? They'll probably break up and get back together at least two more times before school's out. They're definitely going to set a record."

Sydney snickered and began to refill a napkin dispenser. The best part about her job at the Cineplex in the Division Street Mall was that Emma worked there, too. The two of them had been best friends since sixth grade, but they hadn't been hanging out together much lately.

Probably because I've been seeing so much of Jason, Sydney thought.

Jason Phillips, Sydney's new boyfriend, was not one of Emma's favorite people.

Emma hadn't come right out and said anything, but Sydney could tell. Her friend's blue eyes would practically ice over whenever Jason was around.

Emma just needs a chance to get to know Jason better, Sydney thought. She pushed a strand of dark, curly hair off her forehead.

"Jason's coming to my house later to study for Wednesday's history test. Why don't you come, too?" she suggested. "We could pick up a pizza."

Emma shook her head. "I'd better not. I want to talk to the manager when he comes in later. See if I can get an extra shift here."

Sydney stared at her. "More work? Emma, you already work three evenings a week, plus weekends!"

"Believe me, I know how much I work," Emma said, rolling her eyes. She sighed. "But I have to do something to earn more money. Things are getting really bad."

"What do you mean?"

"It's my mom," Emma explained, tucking her long blond hair behind her ears. "She hurt her knee when she was younger, and it never really healed right. The doctor says she really needs an operation."

Sydney frowned in sympathy. Emma's mother worked as a waitress in the Shadyside Diner. She was on her feet from four to midnight six days a week.

"You mean the diner won't pay her for the time she's out for the operation?" she asked. "Is that why you need extra money?"

Emma snorted. "The diner won't pay her while she's out. And they're going to fire her if she doesn't get her knee fixed soon. They say the customers are starting to complain because she's so slow."

"That's rotten!" Sydney declared.

"Tell me about it." Emma sighed again. "Plus, we don't have any insurance, so we have to pay for the operation ourselves. And we can't unless I find a way to make more money!"

Before Sydney could reply, a man with four little kids rushed up to the counter. As she and Emma scooped popcorn into tubs and filled soda cups, Sydney kept glancing over at her friend.

Emma looks so worried, she thought. So desperate. And no wonder!

Imagine if my own mother needed an operation and couldn't pay for it.

Sydney shook her head. She couldn't imagine it. Not really.

Even though she and Emma were best friends, they were very different. Emma was short and blond. Sydney was tall, with dark-brown hair and eyes.

Sydney was a bundle of nerves, while Emma usually stayed calm and cool about things.

But they also came from totally different worlds.

Sydney's parents had been happily married for twenty years. Emma's parents were divorced, and almost never saw each other.

Emma lived in a tiny, run-down house in the Old Village. Sydney's sprawling mansion sat on five acres of land in North Hills, where everybody had plenty of money.

Emma works because she has to, Sydney thought. I work because Mom and Dad don't want me to be spoiled. They want me to learn responsibility.

Not that Sydney minded. She thought it was a good idea. And she liked her job. But she knew she could walk away from it without worrying about how to pay for food or clothes. Or operations.

A loud shriek interrupted Sydney's thoughts.

One of the little kids she'd just served had tripped and dropped his giant tub of popcorn. Now he was standing in front of the ticket taker, crying and complaining and blocking everybody's way.

Grabbing the broom and dustpan, Sydney sped out from behind the counter while Emma served the customers waiting in line. By the time Sydney finished cleaning up the mountain of popcorn, the concession line was three people deep. She and Emma barely had a chance to breathe until their counter shift was over.

Finally, at five o'clock, they were free. Well, almost free. First they had to empty the trash barrels.

Struggling with three bulging plastic bags, Sydney followed Emma out a side exit to an alley behind the mall.

"This alley gives me the creeps," Sydney declared with a shudder. They walked toward the big metal garbage bins. "It's always so dark."

"Yeah, and the Dumpsters stink," Emma complained. She heaved her trash bags into one of them.

Sydney swung her arms and tossed her bags up toward the top of the bin. Two of them fell in. The third one caught on the edge.

As Sydney reached up to push it over, her silver charm bracelet snagged on the bin's sharp corner. She tugged gently. But not gently enough.

The clasp broke. The bracelet began to slide off her wrist. Sydney made a frantic grab for it.

Missed.

The bracelet skittered over the edge of the bin and dropped inside.

Gasping, Sydney stuck her hand over the top of the bin and reached down. All she felt was the smooth plastic of the trash bags.

"What are you *doing?*" Emma demanded.

"My charm bracelet fell in!" Sydney cried.

"Oh, no! The sterling silver one?" Emma asked.

Sydney nodded. "It's been in our family forever. My grandmother gave it to me."

She glanced around the shadowy alley and spotted a stack of cinder blocks against the back wall. "Help me carry some of those over here, would you?"

Emma wrinkled her nose. "You're not going to dig through the garbage, are you?"

"I have to," Sydney told her. "I absolutely have to get that bracelet back! It's my favorite thing in the world!"

With Emma's help, Sydney stacked two of the rough cinder blocks next to the rusting Dumpster. Then she climbed up to peer inside.

"See it?" Emma asked.

Sydney shook her head. "It probably slid under the bags we just threw in." She grabbed one of the bags and carefully moved it aside. Underneath it lay another bag, split open and spilling out a mound of ripe, smelly garbage.

"Gross." Sydney held her breath and reached for a corner of the second bag.

The bag rustled and shifted.

And then it suddenly was heaved into the air as if it had been punched from below.

"Something's in here!" Sydney screamed. "Something alive!"

chapter
2

 S ydney snatched her hand away and screamed again.

Two eyes glared up at her from behind a wad of crumpled napkins.

Two angry eyes in a face of mud-brown fur, long whiskers, and sharp, gleaming teeth.

"A rat!" she cried. "Oh, gross, Emma! It's a rat!"

"Get away—quick!" Emma exclaimed.

Before Sydney could move, the rat jumped up, its claws scrabbling on the metal lip of the dumpster. It uttered a catlike hiss and s jaws.

Sydney gasped and stumbled blocks.

With another hiss, the rat le bin. Emma gasped and bac

The rat paused for a moment and stared at the two girls as if trying to decide whether to attack them. Then it turned away and scurried down the alley, its hairless tail dragging behind it.

Emma let her breath out. "Ohhh. I feel sick. I really do. That thing was huge!"

"Yeah. Let's hope none of its friends are down in the bin," Sydney replied. With a shudder, she started to climb back up on the blocks.

Emma's eyes widened. "Sydney! You're not going to keep looking in there, are you?"

"I have to," Sydney declared. "I really have to find that bracelet, Emma." She gave her friend a pleading look. "I'll find it a lot faster if you help."

Emma groaned. But with Sydney's help, she dragged some more blocks over to the bin. Then they both climbed up and peered inside.

Covering her nose and mouth with one hand, Sydney reached down and shoved some garbage away. Beneath it was more garbage—orange peels, rotting hot dog buns, grease-soaked papers.

"I wish we had gloves," she muttered. She lifted some papers between two fingers and tossed them aside. "When I get home, I'm going to wash my hands for an hour!"

"I wish we had oxygen masks," Emma grumbled. She sighed and tossed a garbage bag from one side of the bin to the other. "The manager is probably here now, Syd. I have to talk to him, remember?"

"I know. But he'll be here for a while," Sydney told her. "This won't take that long. I mean, I *know* the bracelet's here somewhere. I saw it fall in."

Emma picked up a popcorn tub, peered into it, then tossed it away. "Let's just hope it didn't fall all the way to the bottom. I want to help you, Syd. But . . . *no way* am I climbing into this thing."

Using a stick she'd found in the bin, Sydney flipped over a mound of trash.

"Emma!" she cried, pointing. "I see it!"

"Grab it quick, Syd—and let's get out of here," Emma groaned.

Glinting in the dim light, the antique silver charm bracelet lay on top of a tan duffel bag. Sydney bent over the edge of the bin and stretched her fingers down. She caught one end of the bracelet and pulled.

The bracelet started to slither free, then caught on something.

"It's stuck," Sydney announced. "Stuck on some kind of bag." She grabbed a handle and hauled the greasy duffel bag up and over the side of the bin.

With a sigh of relief, Sydney hopped down and sat on the cement blocks. She set the bag on her lap and carefully untwisted her bracelet. As she did, the bag toppled to the ground.

Sydney glanced at it, then down at the bracelet. Something caught her eye.

Poking from the bag's partly opened zipper was the corner of a bill.

"Is that what I think it is?" Sydney asked. "It looks like a fifty-dollar bill."

"Huh?" Emma grabbed the bag and yanked the zipper all the way open.

"Is it?" Sydney asked, busy with the clasp on her bracelet.

Emma remained silent.

Sydney clasped the bracelet around her wrist and glanced at her friend. "Well? Is it a fifty-dollar bill?"

Emma raised her eyes from the bag. "You're not going to believe this," she whispered. She pulled the bag open wide. "Look!"

Sydney peered into the bag. "Whoa!"

Stacks and stacks of bills. Wrapped in rubber bands.

Fifty-dollar bills.

"I don't believe it!" Emma cried excitedly. She picked up one of the stacks and riffled it like a deck of cards. "They're *all* fifties!"

Emma grabbed another stack and riffled through it. So did Sydney. In minutes, stacks of fifty-dollar bills were spread out at their feet.

"Wow. I mean, *wow!* It's at least a hundred thousand dollars!" Emma whispered.

"Unreal." Sydney stared at it, then at Emma. "Whose is it, do you think? What's it doing in the Dumpster?"

Emma slowly shook her head. "A hundred thousand dollars," she murmured again, not taking her eyes off the money. "A hundred thousand dollars!"

chapter

3

Sydney frowned at the stacks of money. "This is really weird, to say the least. What do you think it was doing in the Dumpster?" she repeated.

"Who cares?" Emma glanced around the alley. Then she quickly began to stuff the stacks of fifties back into the bag. "We'd better hide it before anybody sees us with it."

"You're right," Sydney agreed. "Do you think it's from a bank robbery or something?"

Emma shrugged.

"Maybe the police will know." Sydney closed the zipper and laughed. "I can't wait to see the expression on their faces when we hand it to them."

"Are you serious?" Emma asked. "You really want to hand all this money over to the police?"

"Sure. I mean, what else can we do?"

Emma leaned close, her blue eyes blazing with excitement. "Keep it!" she whispered.

Sydney stared at her friend. "You're kidding, right?" She waited for Emma to laugh, to tell her she was joking. But Emma didn't even crack a smile.

She *isn't* kidding, Sydney thought. She really means it.

"Think about it, Syd!" Emma urged. "We can split it—fifty thousand dollars each! I could pay for Mom's operation! We could finally get our roof fixed and buy a new—"

"Whoa!" Sydney cut her off. "How would you explain to your mother where you suddenly got fifty thousand dollars?"

"I'd tell her the truth," Emma declared. "Mom wouldn't care. Why should she?"

"Because . . ." Sydney paused, shaking her head. She couldn't believe Emma actually wanted to do this. "Look, I don't want to sound like a goody-goody. But, Emma, it's not ours!"

"Sure it is!" Emma cried. "It was buried under a pile of garbage inside a Dumpster—and *we* found it. Finders, keepers. Right?"

"But . . ."

"Come on, Sydney! Anybody else would keep it. Why shouldn't we?" Emma demanded. "You know what else I could do with this money? I could go to college. I wouldn't have to worry about getting that scholarship anymore. And I could buy some decent clothes!"

Sydney's eyes widened in surprise. "What's the matter with your clothes?"

"I wear the same things every day." Emma sighed. "It's embarrassing. But you wouldn't know about that," she added bitterly. "You don't understand what it's like to be really poor. What it's like to want something you can't have. But *I* do. And I'm telling you, we've *got* to keep this money!"

Sydney gazed at her, stunned. Has Emma always resented me for being rich? she wondered. Did I just not see it? I never made a big deal about having money. I never bragged about myself or put her down for being poor. I wouldn't do that to anybody—especially to my best friend!

Confused and hurt, Sydney stared at the greasy duffel bag. "You're wrong about one thing," she murmured. "I *do* know what it's like to want things I can't have. My parents don't give me everything I want, you know."

"Oh? Didn't you want a car for your birthday?" Emma asked. "And didn't they give you one?"

"Yes. But I have to pay the insurance on it," Sydney pointed out. "Mom and Dad don't want me to get spoiled, and they keep me on a really tight budget. There are plenty of things I'd like to buy with this money."

"So let's keep it!" Emma cried. "What's stopping us?"

Sydney bit her lip. She had to admit, it was tempting. But scary, too.

"We don't know where it came from," she said. "The police might be looking for it. Or whoever left it here. If we suddenly go on a major shopping binge, and they find out, we could be in major trouble."

Emma thought for a minute. "Okay—here's what we'll do. We won't spend it for a while. We'll hide it someplace and wait and see if there's anything about it on the news."

"And if there is, we turn it in—right?" Sydney asked.

"Yeah. But if there isn't . . ." Emma grinned. "Then it's all ours."

Sydney let out a nervous laugh. She couldn't believe she was actually agreeing to this!

"Where should we hide it?" Emma asked. "Your place? You have that huge attic."

"No! I don't want it in my house," Sydney protested. "I'd be too scared."

"Well, I don't want it at mine, either," Emma said. "Okay, help me think of a good place. Someplace nobody would think of but us."

"How about the old willow tree?" Sydney suggested. "The one in the Fear Street Woods where we used to meet and have picnics and stuff."

"Perfect!" Emma agreed. "We can bury it under the tree. Nobody will ever know. Then we'll just hang out for a couple of weeks until we're sure it's safe to dig it up."

Sydney glanced around. Daylight was fading fast. The shadowy alley had grown even darker. She shivered and rubbed her arms. "Let's get out of here."

"Right." Emma rose and picked up the duffel bag. "Can you drive us to the woods?"

"Sure. Let's just do it, okay?"

As they started out of the alley, Sydney turned and glanced back. It's not too late, she thought. Take the bag and throw it back in the Dumpster. Let somebody else find it.

"Come on, Syd!" Emma urged, giggling with excitement. "Hurry!"

Sydney paused for a second longer. Then, taking a deep breath, she followed her friend out of the alley.

"There it is!" Emma cried, pointing.

Sydney gazed along the path that wound through the Fear Street Woods.

Several yards ahead stood an enormous willow tree. Its lower branches drooped to the ground, forming a pale-green curtain.

We used to sit under there and tell secrets, Sydney thought. It was the perfect hideaway. Now it's going to hide our biggest secret ever.

Carrying the folding snow shovel from her car trunk, Sydney followed Emma along the muddy path toward the tree.

"The ground is soft," Emma declared as she pulled aside some branches and ducked under.

15

"It'll be easy to dig. I'll go first." She set the bag down and took the shovel from Sydney. She's so excited, Sydney thought. All she talked about on the way here was the stuff she can buy with the money. Her mom's operation. A CD player. Lots of clothes. She's too excited to be scared.

Sydney glanced through the curtain of willow branches. Fear Lake wasn't far from here. She could hear the water lapping at the shore, but she couldn't see it. The Fear Street Woods were tangled and overgrown. And dark.

Sydney shivered. She wished she'd never thought of bringing the money here.

She reached for the shovel. "I'll dig now." She jammed it into the hole Emma had started and began shoveling. Before long, the hole was about two feet deep.

Emma lowered the bag inside, and Sydney quickly scraped the dirt back over it. Emma set a sand-colored stone on top as a marker, then brushed the dirt off her hands.

"Two weeks," she said with a satisfied smile. "If nothing happens, we'll come back and get it in two weeks."

"Okay. But let's go now," Sydney urged, folding up the shovel. "These woods are creeping me out."

As they started back to the car, Sydney suddenly stopped and grabbed Emma's arm. "Wait!" she whispered. "Did you hear that?"

"What?"

"I'm not sure." Sydney held her breath, listening.

A twig snapped. Leaves rustled. The sounds came from behind them.

Emma's eyes widened in fear as another twig cracked. Closer now.

Sydney's heart pounded in her ears. Did somebody see us bury that bag? Maybe somebody followed us from the alley.

Leaves rustled again. Louder. Closer.

Gasping in fear, Sydney turned to look.

And screamed as a dark shape leaped onto the path.

chapter
4

Sydney stumbled into Emma. And screamed again.

"Stop it, Sydney!" Emma cried, using Sydney's arm to steady herself. "It's just a raccoon!"

Sydney clamped her hand over her mouth and stared down at the dark, furry creature. The raccoon gazed back for a moment, its dark-ringed eyes bright with fear. Then it shuffled off the path and disappeared into the tangled undergrowth.

Sydney let her breath out in relief. "I thought—I thought somebody watched us bury the money!"

"Me, too," Emma admitted. She pushed her long, blond hair back and laughed. "Come on. Let's get out of here before we both turn totally paranoid."

Sydney took one final glance at the willow tree.

Its drooping branches swayed like a curtain in the breeze. With a shudder, Sydney turned and hurried away.

Sydney dropped Emma off at her house, then drove home as fast as she could. Her hands were grimy from digging through the Dumpster. Her fingernails had crescents of dirt under them. Thick mud coated her sneakers.

A long, hot shower, she thought. That's what I need now.

But Sydney knew it would take more than a shower to get rid of her doubts. Why had she let Emma talk her into taking that money?

Emma could really use it, she knew that. And it wasn't like they'd stolen it.

Was it?

Edgy and still worried, Sydney turned her red Miata between the tall, iron gates and started up the long, curving drive to her rambling stone house. She followed the drive around to the back, a cobblestone courtyard with a long row of horse stables.

Since they only had two horses, three of the stables had been converted into garages. Sydney's father parked his BMW in the first one. As she rolled toward the second one, she braked suddenly.

The door to her father's garage stood open.

A figure bent over the engine of her dad's car, the yellow garage light glowing on his thick, sandy hair.

Jason Phillips. Sydney's boyfriend.

I totally forgot, she thought. We're supposed to study together. No way will I be able to concentrate, not after what I've just done.

She smiled as Jason waved at her. At least he didn't get bored waiting. Give him a car to fix, and Jason was happy.

Sydney waved back, then pulled the Miata into its garage. Tilting the rearview mirror, she checked her face and hair. Dirt smeared her cheeks and chin. A couple of leaves had caught in her hair. She wiped her face with a tissue, picked out the leaves, and hurried over to Jason.

"Sorry I'm so late. What's wrong with Dad's car?"

"The spark plugs needed changing. I decided to take care of it while I was waiting." Jason peered over the hood at her. Tall and good-looking, he had blue eyes that crinkled at the corners when he smiled.

But he wasn't smiling now. "What happened to you?" he asked. "I was getting worried."

"Oh, I . . ." Sydney groped around for an excuse. "I had to work late. Somebody didn't show up."

She felt her face get hot and knew she was blushing. She always blushed when she lied.

"Come on, Sydney, I'm not exactly an idiot," he told her. "If you were working late, you would have called. And you didn't."

Sydney twisted a strand of hair around her finger and tried to think of what to say.

Jason narrowed his eyes. "You're hiding something," he declared. "I can see it in your face."

"I'm not. . . ."

"Yes, you are!" Jason slammed the car hood down with a bang.

Sydney jumped, feeling a twinge of fear at that blazing look in his eyes.

"What's your secret, Sydney?" Jason demanded. "Another guy? Were you out seeing somebody else while I waited here like an idiot?"

"No!"

"Then tell me the truth." Jason skirted the car and strode over to her. "Where were you? What were you doing?"

She stared hard at Jason, frightened and confused.

Should I try to come up with another lie?

Or should I tell him about the money?

chapter
5

"If you weren't out with another guy, then tell me where you were," Jason insisted.

Sydney remained silent, still trying to decide.

Jason's shoulders sagged. "I guess I have my answer," he muttered.

He started to stride away.

"No!" Sydney reached out and grabbed his hand. "It's not what you think, Jason. It really isn't! I'll tell you, okay? But you have to promise not to tell anybody."

"Why?"

"Just promise!" she insisted.

"Okay, okay. I promise." Twisting his fingers through hers, Jason led her to the workbench at the back of the garage. He took a can of soda from a small cooler, popped the top, and handed it to her.

"Thanks." Sydney took a long drink.

Jason reached out and touched her hair, pulling part of a leaf from one of the dark curls. "You look like you've been on a hike," he remarked.

He kissed her softly, then leaned back against the workbench. "Okay," he said. "Tell me."

"I have been on a hike, sort of."

Sydney took another gulp of soda, then fingered the silver charm bracelet on her wrist. "It all started with this," she added.

Taking a deep breath, Sydney told Jason the story—her bracelet falling into the Dumpster, the disgusting garbage, the rat. And the grease-stained duffel bag filled with fifty-dollar bills.

Jason stared at her, an amazed expression on his face. "A hundred thousand dollars?" he asked slowly. "Whooooa! Are you sure?"

Sydney nodded. "Maybe more. We were too excited to really count it."

Jason whistled softly.

"The whole thing felt so unreal!" she went on. "Like something from a movie!"

"What happened next?"

"Emma got really pumped."

Jason laughed. "No kidding?"

"Well, you know she has hardly any money, Jason," Sydney reminded him.

"She's not the only one."

23

"Oh, come on," Sydney argued. "Your family's not dripping with money, maybe. But you have enough and you know it."

"Okay. Forget that." Jason popped open another can of soda and took a drink. "What happened next?"

"I wanted to turn it in to the police," Sydney went on. "But then Emma started talking about all the things she could use it for. And I started to get excited, too. We argued a little. But finally, we decided to keep the money. To take it and hide it."

Sydney told Jason about burying the bag of money under the willow tree in the Fear Street Woods. When she finished, she almost laughed in relief. It felt so good to tell somebody what they'd done!

Jason whistled again. Then he leaned forward, his eyes intense. "Okay, listen," he said. "Are you sure nobody else was in that alley?"

"Just Emma and me. And the rat." Sydney shuddered. "You should have seen that gross, disgusting rat, Jason! It was as big as . . ."

"You didn't spot anyone on your way out?" he interrupted. "Nobody followed you to the woods?"

"I'm positive nobody did."

Jason nodded to himself. "Tell me again about the money," he said. "Who actually found it? You or Emma?"

"Well, I found the bag," Sydney told him. "And I

24

thought I saw a bill sticking out of it. Then Emma opened it and saw all the money." She frowned at him. "Why did you ask that question?"

"It's just too bad that Emma opened the bag." Jason paused, and a strange smile spread over his face. "Now the only way you and I can split up the money is to murder her."

chapter

6

"*E*xcuse me?" Sydney gasped. Had she heard him right? She couldn't have! "What did you say?"

"I said if you and I are going to split the money, we'll have to kill Emma," Jason repeated.

"Whooooa." Sydney stared at him, shocked.

"Didn't you see that movie?" Jason asked. "These four guys find a bag filled with cash. They decide to keep it. And then they all start killing each other to make sure the secret is safe."

"I never saw it," Sydney told him.

"Great movie." Jason grinned.

A feeling of relief washed over Sydney. "I thought you were serious for a second," she told him. "I mean, about killing Emma."

Jason's blue eyes widened in surprise. "Is that what you think of me?"

Sydney didn't know what to say. She laughed, feeling embarrassed.

Finding the money has made me really paranoid, she scolded herself.

Jason shook his head. "I was talking about a movie, Sydney. You know—fantasy land?" He pulled her close and kissed her again. "Of course I wasn't serious!"

Monday afternoon, footsteps echoed loudly in the long, tiled halls of Shadyside High as students hurried to their final class.

Pushed along by the crowd, Sydney searched through the notebooks she carried. Where was her chemistry homework? She'd brought it to school, hadn't she?

Stepping out of the moving tide of kids, she leaned against a wall and checked her notebooks again. The homework wasn't there.

She must have left it in her locker. Now she'd have to go all the way downstairs to get it.

Sydney sighed in frustration. She'd been messing up the entire day.

She hadn't slept all night. And she'd forgotten to set her alarm, so she had to rush to school. No chance to comb her hair until after first period.

At lunch, she'd dumped her entire tray, including the silverware, into the garbage can.

She'd totally forgotten about the quiz in English and had to wing it.

It's the money, Sydney told herself as she shoved her way back into the crowded hallway. It's turning me into a nervous wreck!

"Sydney, wait up!" a voice called from behind her.

Glancing over her shoulder, Sydney saw Emma making her way toward her. They didn't have any classes together—not even lunch—so it was the first time she'd seen Emma all day.

Emma doesn't look like she's ready to freak, Sydney thought. She looks happy. Excited. Probably slept great. Dreamed about giving her mom the money for the operation and then going on a major shopping trip.

"Hi!" Emma cried breathlessly, finally catching up to Sydney. "Guess what?"

"What?"

"I actually read the newspaper this morning!" Emma's blue eyes sparkled. "No news," she announced, her voice full of meaning.

Sydney glanced around. "I really don't think we should talk about it here, okay?"

Emma laughed. "Lighten up, Sydney. All I said was I read the newspaper. Nobody's paying attention, anyway."

"You're right. I'm just nervous," Sydney replied.

"Well, relax." Emma nudged her in the side.

"And keep your fingers crossed. In thirteen more days, if nothing comes up, we'll be home free!"

Sydney nodded and forced a smile as the crowd pushed them toward the head of the stairs. She hoped Emma wouldn't talk about it anymore.

She and Emma started down the stairs. Another large group of kids swept in behind them. A noisy group, talking loudly and excitedly about the upcoming basketball game.

One of them jostled Sydney from behind and her foot slipped. "Hey!" she cried, grabbing hold of the banister to steady herself.

Another wild burst of laughter erupted.

And then a piercing scream rang out.

Sydney turned to her left, just in time to see Emma's arms flail out. Her hands grabbed at nothing but air.

She's falling! Sydney realized.

Clinging to the banister with one hand, Sydney threw out her free arm to catch her friend.

Too late.

With a terrified scream, Emma shot forward like a diver and tumbled headfirst down the steep concrete stairs.

"Emma!" Sydney cried.

Emma hit the middle steps with a sickening *thud*. Then bumped and rolled all the way to the bottom.

Students starting up the stairs jumped aside, crying out in surprise. Emma landed in a heap at their feet.

"Emma!" Sydney called. In a panic, she started down, but someone blocked her way. Then someone else bumped her from the side, slamming her hard against the banister.

Gasping, she glanced up, at the top of the stairs.

Jason stood there, staring down. Not at Sydney. At Emma.

Sydney could see his teeth, white and gleaming. And his eyes, crinkling at the corners.

Was that a grin on Jason's face? Was he actually smiling?

No, of course not, she told herself. Jason wouldn't smile at a time like this. It's the light. The shadows. Something!

Anxious to get to her friend, Sydney turned away from Jason and charged down the stairs.

A crowd of kids huddled in a tight circle at the bottom of the steps, staring down in horror.

They're so quiet, Sydney thought. Why aren't they helping Emma up? Why aren't they calling for help?

Pushing her way through the knot of students, Sydney finally caught a glimpse of her friend.

Emma lay sprawled on her stomach, her arms flung out above her head.

Her long blond hair spilled over the floor.

She's so still, Sydney thought.

Dropping to her knees, Sydney gently pushed the hair away from Emma's face. "Emma?" she whispered.

Emma didn't move.

"Emma?" Sydney touched her friend's back. "Emma."

Nothing. No movement at all.

"She's not breathing!" Sydney wailed. "She's dead!"

chapter
7

"I can't believe she didn't even break anything!" Sydney exclaimed for about the tenth time. "Are you sure she's going to be all right?"

Dr. Lasher nodded briskly and folded his stethoscope into his bag. "She'll be sore for a few days from the bruising," he told her. "And her head is probably going to ache some. But there's no concussion. Nothing to worry about."

He smiled at her. "Try to relax, Sydney. Your friend is fine."

Still shaken, Sydney collapsed on a faded, lumpy armchair in the living room of Emma's house.

She knew she'd never forget the sight of her friend, lying so still at the bottom of those stairs! Sydney knew it was only a couple of seconds until

Emma finally took a breath. But it had felt like hours.

And then Emma's eyes opened, and she was sitting up, trying to get to her feet. The school nurse checked her over thoroughly. She was badly shaken but seemed okay.

So Sydney had driven Emma home, then called her own family doctor to come check her out. Now Emma was dozing in the bedroom, and Emma's mother had left for work.

"Here." Dr. Lasher held out a couple of freezable gel-packs. "Put these in the freezer. She can use them on that left shoulder. It's going to give her some pain."

Thanking him again, Sydney let the doctor out. Then she shut the door and gazed around the living room.

Clean, but dark and faded, the room held a foldout couch where Emma's mother slept, two old easy chairs, and a bulky old television.

A plastic bucket with an inch of water in it stood in one corner. The roof leaks, Sydney remembered with a sigh.

"Sydney?" Emma's voice called from the bedroom.

"You're awake! Just a sec." Sydney strode into the kitchen and put the gel-packs in the freezer compartment of the refrigerator. Then she hurried down the short hall to the house's only bedroom.

Emma had tried to brighten up the room with

movie posters on the walls and a yellow rug on the floor. But with only one small window, it stayed dim and shadowy.

"How do you feel?" Sydney asked. "Want some aspirin? Or maybe something to eat or drink?"

Emma shook her head. "Not now. Thanks," she murmured.

Sydney crossed the room and sat down on the edge of the bed. "You sure?"

"I'm okay." Emma shoved her hair back and closed her eyes, frowning.

"That's exactly what Dr. Lasher said—that you're okay," Sydney told her, trying to sound cheerful. "You don't look bad, either," she added. "Kind of pale. But definitely not like you just fell down a bunch of stairs."

Emma's eyes snapped open. Jamming the pillow behind her back, she eased herself up into a sitting position and gazed intently at Sydney.

"I didn't fall, Syd," she declared.

"What? What do you mean?"

"Somebody pushed me."

"Pushed you? Are you sure?" Sydney demanded.

"You want to know who?" Emma asked. "Jason."

chapter

8

"*H*uh?" Sydney stared at her. "No way! That's impossible! He . . . ."

"I saw him behind me," Emma told her. "Then I felt his hands on my shoulders. I thought he was just kidding around, but then I realized I was wrong."

Her lips twisted in a bitter smile. "I mean, Jason and I aren't exactly buddies. We don't kid around."

Sydney shook her head. She didn't believe this!

"I felt his hands," Emma continued in a shaky voice. "And then he—he pushed me down the stairs!"

"No!" Sydney rose from the bed. "That's *crazy!*"

"Is it?" Emma sat up straighter. "Let me ask you something, Sydney. Did you tell Jason about the money we found?"

"Emma—what does that have to do with anything?" Sydney cried.

"Just answer," Emma demanded. "Did you tell him about the bag of money?"

"Yes! Okay, I told him!" Sydney admitted. Her face flushed with guilt. "I wasn't going to say a word. But when I got back from the woods yesterday, he saw that something was wrong. He asked where I'd been. And I made up this dumb story about working late. Surprise, surprise—he didn't believe me."

"Yeah. You're a lousy liar," Emma agreed.

"Then he got angry. Really angry," Sydney continued. "He thought I'd been out with another guy. I didn't want him to think that. And besides, I still felt weird about what we'd done."

"So you told him the truth?" Emma demanded, narrowing her eyes at Sydney.

Sydney nodded.

"Did you tell him where we hid the money, too?"

Sydney nodded. "Everything. I'm sorry, I know I promised not to. But Emma, you're wrong about him pushing you. He wouldn't do something like that! Why would he?"

"Are you kidding?" Emma asked skeptically. "For the money!"

"No way!" Sydney argued. "Jason is not poor. His family has enough money!"

"Not enough for him," Emma declared. "Remember those sneakers he wanted? The hundred-

and-fifty-dollar ones? He already had a perfectly good pair, but he hinted and hinted about those others until you went out and bought them for him!"

"So what?"

"So he's greedy!" Emma shot back. "You know he is, Syd. He's always talking you into buying him things. Like that beeper. And that CD player for his car. He's not poor—he's greedy!"

"No." Sydney crossed her arms and shook her head violently. "No!"

"Yes," Emma insisted. "And that's why he pushed me. To try to kill me. I bet he *would* kill me for my share of the money!"

Emma is not making sense, Sydney thought desperately. Nothing she says is making sense!

"Emma, listen. You just fell down a steep stairway. A cement one. You must have hit your head harder than the doctor says, because you're not thinking clearly! What you said about Jason is totally crazy!"

Emma's eyes flashed, but she didn't reply.

Sydney turned and gazed out the window. The beat-up old VW that Emma's uncle had given her stood on the narrow strip of gravel at the side of the house. As Sydney stared at it, an image of Jason crept into her mind.

Jason, as he stood at the top of the school stairs only a couple of hours before.

His eyes, crinkled at the corners, gazing down at Emma.

His teeth bared in a grin.

The same strange grin Sydney had seen last night, when he talked about killing Emma.

But he was just talking about a movie! Sydney thought. He said he was kidding!

But was he kidding? she wondered with a shiver. Did Jason really try to kill Emma?

chapter
9

*F*rowning, Sydney hurried through the hallway at school the next morning. She didn't have much time. The bell between classes would ring in another minute.

She had to talk to him now. Had to find out why he stood there with a grin on his face while Emma crashed to the bottom of the stairs.

Emma is so sure he pushed her, Sydney thought. Is she wrong? Or did Jason really try to kill her for her share of the money?

Sydney shuddered. She wished they'd never found that stupid money! She'd hardly slept for two nights, worrying about it. And now she had to confront her boyfriend and find out if he tried to kill somebody because of it!

As Sydney rounded the corner, the bell rang. She planted herself across the hall from the computer lab and eyed the students as they started to pour through the door.

Jason was the third one out. He kept his head down as he stuffed some papers into his backpack and started to join the flow of kids in the hallway.

"Jason!" Sydney called.

His head snapped up. His eyes searched the hall. When he spotted her, he smiled.

Sydney swallowed dryly. That couldn't be a killer's smile, she thought. It couldn't!

"Hey, Sydney." Zipping his pack, Jason threaded his way across the crowded hall and joined her. "What's up?"

"I have to talk to you," she told him. "I tried to call you last night, but nobody was home."

"Yeah, we went to my sister's house for dinner." Jason took her hand and pulled her into step beside him. "We can talk on the way to English. What's up?"

Sydney took a shaky breath. "It's about Emma."

Jason's eyes flashed. "What about her? She's all right, isn't she? I mean, she got up and walked away from that fall yesterday, so I . . ."

"She's okay," Sydney interrupted. "Do you really care?"

"Huh? What's that supposed to mean?"

Sydney tugged him out of the crowd and over to the side of the hall. "She says you pushed her down those stairs!" she blurted out. "She says she saw you behind her, Jason! Then she felt your hands on her shoulders. And then, she felt you push her!"

"That's crazy!" Jason angrily slapped a locker. "Emma is totally paranoid!"

"But you *were* on the stairs," Sydney reminded him. "I saw you. She didn't make that up."

"No!"

As Jason ran his fingers through his sandy hair, a faint blush crept across his cheeks. "I was there. In fact, I can sort of guess why Emma thinks I pushed her. See, I tripped. So I stuck out my hands to catch my balance and . . . I bumped into her. I feel terrible about it!"

"Then why were you smiling?" Sydney demanded. "Right after she fell, somebody shoved me against the railing, and I looked back. You were watching her fall, and you had a grin on your face, Jason!"

He shook his head, his blue eyes wide and innocent. "I was shocked, Sydney! I mean, totally blown away! I tried to yell, but I couldn't make a sound. My whole face sort of froze. Maybe I looked like I was smiling. But I wasn't!"

Sydney gazed at him for a moment, then slumped against the bank of lockers. The whole thing had been an accident, she realized in relief.

"Jason, I'm sorry," she murmured. "I've just been so upset and nervous. I didn't mean to accuse you."

41

"Don't worry about it." He smiled and kissed her forehead. "No problem, Syd. Really. Like I said, I can see why Emma thought I pushed her."

"You should tell her, you know. Clear things up and apologize. I mean, you did make her fall, even though it wasn't on purpose," Sydney said.

"You think she'll believe me?" he asked. "She hates my guts!"

"But if you tell her exactly what happened, she'll understand," Sydney argued. "Look, I know you two aren't crazy about each other. But you really should tell her. Who knows? Maybe you'll actually become friends."

"Don't count on it." Jason sighed. He fiddled with the zipper on his backpack for a second. Then he shrugged. "You're right. I should tell her what happened."

"Good."

He grinned. "I'll try to make it up to her. She's been complaining about that junky car of hers. So I'll see what I can do to get it running better. And I'll do it for free—how's that?"

"Great!" Sydney threw her arms around his neck and gave him another kiss. "Thanks, Jason!"

Jason hurried off to his English class. Sydney breathed another sigh of relief. Emma made a mistake, that's all, she told herself. Jason would never try to kill someone for money!

* * *

Later that afternoon, Sydney sat on her bed studying for a history test and snacking on taco chips. As she stuck her hand into the bag for another chip, her bedside phone rang.

"Hello?"

"You'll never guess what happened," Emma announced.

Sydney licked the salt from her fingers. "Tell me."

"Jason just left my house, and my car is actually purring like a kitten!"

"No kidding? That's great!" Sydney smiled to herself. Jason had come through.

"Yeah, and guess what else?" Emma asked. "He didn't charge me for it. Plus, he explained to me how he tripped on the stairs and bumped into me, and that's why I fell." She laughed. "I couldn't believe it—the guy actually felt guilty!"

"Of course he did," Sydney declared. "He told me about it at school today. He feels really terrible."

"I bet he does. And after he fixed my car and didn't get paid for it, I bet he feels even worse."

"Emma!"

"Sorry. And listen—I'm sorry I accused him, Sydney," Emma said. "I was really stressed out. I still am. That bruise on my shoulder is the color of an eggplant. And I keep getting headaches."

"Dr. Lasher said you might," Sydney replied. "It's good you stayed home from school today. Maybe you'll feel better tomorrow."

43

"I hope so." Emma sighed. "But anyway, I'm still really excited about the money. I can hardly believe it's ours! Just think, Syd! Pretty soon we'll be able to actually spend it!"

"Mmm." Sydney still felt uncomfortable talking about it.

"Hey, why don't we go to the mall?" Emma suggested. "We can window-shop for all the stuff we're going to buy!"

"Well . . ." Sydney hesitated. "What about your headache? I thought you didn't feel well."

"I don't. But going to the mall will make me feel much better," Emma replied. "Please, Sydney? It'll be fun."

Sydney glanced down at her history book. She wasn't finished studying, but it was her best subject. Besides, they wouldn't actually be spending the money. "Okay. Sure. I'll come pick you up."

"Nope. *I'll* drive," Emma told her with a laugh. "I want to see the miracles Jason did to my car. Oh, wait," she added. "I have to stick around. I promised my neighbor I'd make sure her kids get home from the bus stop okay. It won't be too long. Why don't you drive over to my house? Then we'll take my car to the mall."

"Okay. See you in a few minutes." Sydney hung up and scooted off the bed. As she did, the phone rang again.

"Getting sick of history?" Jason asked. "Ready for a break?"

"Actually, I was just about to take one," Sydney

told him. "Emma and I are going to the mall. And she's driving, thanks to you." She laughed. "She's really happy about her car, Jason. Thanks for . . ."

"Wait a sec," he interrupted. *"Emma* is driving?"

"That's what I said."

"Why?" Jason demanded. "You guys always take *your* car when you're together."

"I know. But since hers is running now, she . . ." Sydney broke off, frowning. "What difference does it make, anyway?"

"Uh . . . well . . ." Jason paused. "Listen, why don't I pick you up and we'll go somewhere? You can see Emma some other time."

"Jason!" Sydney laughed. "I'm practically on my way out the door. Emma is waiting for me."

"Call her and cancel," he said.

What is the matter with him? Sydney wondered. "We won't be gone long. I'll call you when I get back."

As Jason started to protest again, Sydney heard her mother's voice in the downstairs hall. "Listen, I've got to go," she told him. "Mom just got home and I have to give her a couple of phone messages. Talk to you later!"

Downstairs, Sydney gave her mother the messages and told her where she was going. Then she hopped in her car and drove over to Emma's house.

Emma sat waiting for her on the cracked concrete steps. As Sydney got out of the Miata, Emma jumped up, dangling her car keys from her finger. "Ready for a test drive?"

"Sure." Sydney grinned and followed her over to the scratched, brown VW.

"It doesn't look any better," Emma told her as they slid into the front seat. "But it sounds fantastic. Listen!"

Emma turned the key, and the motor roared to life. Laughing excitedly, she put it in gear and pulled onto the road. Bouncing over potholes, she drove through the narrow streets of the Old Village. Then she turned onto Division Street.

"Now we can really see what kind of job Jason did!" she cried. She drove the car smoothly around a wide curve, then gunned it up a steep hill. "Hey, it's actually climbing the hill! I can't believe it!"

Sydney laughed and turned on the radio. Static crackled through the speakers. "Next time, get Jason to fix the radio," she suggested, turning it off.

"Ha! Maybe there won't be any next time," Emma declared as the car crested a steep hill. "Maybe I'll just take my share of the money and buy myself a cool *new* car!"

The car picked up speed as it started down the hill. Trees and bushes turned into blurs of green. The tires whined on the pavement as the car zoomed down the hill.

At the bottom was a four-way stop.

Emma sighed and touched her foot to the brake.

The car didn't slow.

"Emma?" Sydney gazed ahead at the stop sign. "Better slow down."

"I'm trying." Emma pushed the brake again, harder.

Nothing.

"Emma, slow down!" Sydney shouted.

"I can't!"

Emma frantically pumped the pedal.

"I can't stop the car! The brakes are out!"

chapter
10

The car hurtled down the hill, faster and faster.

Sydney clutched the armrest and gazed in horror at the bottom of the hill.

A silver minivan had paused at the intersection. In another few seconds it would be right in their way. "That van—we're going to crash into it!" she screamed.

Her eyes bulging, Emma pumped the useless brakes. "I can't stop! I can't stop!"

The minivan nosed its way into the intersection. Emma hit the horn and kept her hand on it.

The minivan jerked to a stop. But by now it had reached the middle of the intersection.

Sydney could see the driver's face, frozen in fear

and shock. "Try the emergency brake!" Sydney screamed.

Emma didn't respond.

With one hand on the horn and the other on the steering wheel, she stared straight ahead, her eyes wide with panic.

Sydney reached over, grabbed hold of the emergency brake—and yanked the lever up.

Metal shrieked. Gravel flew. The car bucked and began to skid.

The silver van began to back up.

At the last second, Emma yanked the wheel to the left—and swerved around it. Missed it by inches.

With the horn blaring, the car sailed through the intersection, spun around in a complete circle, and came to a stop on the soft shoulder on the other side of the road.

Shaking all over, Sydney closed her eyes and leaned against the door. As she struggled to catch her breath, she could hear Emma gasping beside her. Sydney's eyes snapped open. Emma sat with her head against the steering wheel. Her arms hung limply at her sides.

"Are you okay?" Sydney asked. "Are you hurt?"

Emma slowly shook her head. "Just scared," she murmured in a shaky voice.

"Me, too." Sydney shuddered. "We were so lucky, Emma. We could have died!"

"I know. That's what he wanted."

Sydney stared at her. "Huh? What do you mean?"

"I was right." Emma raised her head and gazed in horror at Sydney. "Jason *is* trying to kill me. Don't you see? He messed up the brakes. That's why he volunteered to work on my car!"

"No!" Sydney cried. "First you thought he pushed you down the stairs on purpose. Now you're accusing him of messing up the brakes! That's wrong, Emma!"

"Oh?" Emma narrowed her eyes. "There was nothing wrong with the brakes before he fooled around with my car," she said through gritted teeth. "The brakes worked fine. I've been having carburetor problems, not brake trouble!"

"This is an ancient, run-down car," Sydney argued. "The brakes were probably in bad shape, and you just didn't know it."

"You think?" Emma asked doubtfully.

"Of course!" Sydney insisted.

Taking a deep, shaky breath, Emma unbuckled her seat belt and pushed open the driver's door. "I'm going to see if I can tell what went wrong. Then we can hike downtown and call a tow truck."

Still shaken, Sydney twisted a strand of hair around her finger and watched as Emma walked to the front of the car.

The hood rose with a metallic clatter. Emma bent over and peered inside. Then she got down on her knees and disappeared from Sydney's sight for a moment.

What's she doing? Sydney wondered. As she craned her neck, trying to see, Emma suddenly popped up again. "Sydney!" she called sharply.

"What?" Sydney's heart speeded up. "What is it?"

"Come here!" Emma's voice shook with fear again. "You've got to see this!"

Sydney scrambled out of the car, rushed up to Emma, and stared under the hood. "Huh?" she cried, her heart racing. "I don't see anything. What are you showing me?"

chapter

11

"Not there!" Emma told her.

She wrapped her cold fingers around Sydney's wrist and pulled her down to her knees on the gravel.

Then Emma pointed up under the car, near the left front wheel. "Look up there!"

Sydney scrunched down and squinted up at the car.

A long metal tube, not much bigger around than a straw, snaked beneath the wheel well. In the dim light, Sydney could see that it had been sliced clean through.

"What is it?" she asked.

"A brake line," Emma declared.

"Huh? You mean—?"

"And I checked the one on the other side. It's cut, too," Emma declared.

Sydney rose slowly to her feet.

"This wasn't an accident, Sydney," Emma told her grimly. "Someone cut the brake lines."

Sydney gazed at her, horrified. *She means Jason,* she thought.

Not just someone. *Jason!*

Stunned and frightened, Sydney turned away and hurried back inside the car.

Emma climbed in beside her and slammed the door. "You see, don't you?" she asked. "You believe me now? Jason *is* trying to kill me."

Sydney's heart pounded in her chest. She twisted a curl of dark hair around her finger and squeezed her eyes shut. "It's not true!" she cried. "It can't be true!"

"Think about it!" Emma insisted. "We find a pile of money. You tell Jason about it. Then he conveniently bumps into me and knocks me down the stairs. So he 'fixes' my car to make up for it."

She laughed bitterly. "He fixed it, all right. Jason fixed it so well, we almost died!"

Sydney wanted to scream at Emma. Scream that she was wrong. Totally wrong.

But she couldn't say the words. Because maybe, just maybe, Emma was right.

"Jason called me just before I drove over to your house," she said slowly.

Emma's eyes flashed. "Yes?"

"When I told him you were going to drive us to the mall, he sounded . . . weird."

"What do you mean?"

"First, he wanted to know why we were taking your car instead of mine. And then he tried to talk me out of going with you."

Emma punched the steering wheel. "I knew it! I just knew it!"

"If that's really what happened, then he was trying to keep me out of this car," Sydney went on. "Trying to protect me."

Emma laughed bitterly. "Don't kid yourself, Syd. A guy who is that greedy won't share the money with anyone, not even his girlfriend. After he kills me, he'll decide he wants all the money for himself."

"You mean you really think he'd try to . . . kill me next?" Sydney whispered.

Emma nodded. "Count on it."

Sydney stared out the windshield and saw a car cross the intersection. *We could have died there,* she thought with a shiver. *Did Jason sabotage Emma's car?*

She still didn't believe it. Not totally. But she had to find out. She couldn't just pretend that nothing had happened!

"Syd?" Emma's voice broke into Sydney's thoughts. "What do you think we should do?"

"I'll talk to Jason," Sydney replied. "I'll just ask him to his face."

Emma snorted. "Oh, sure! And you think he'll admit it? He'll just deny the whole thing. Put on an innocent expression and lie through his teeth!"

"Then what *can* we do?" Sydney demanded.

"Simple," Emma replied quietly. "Kill *him* first!"

chapter

12

"*E*mma!" Sydney gasped, horrified. "What are you talking about? I can't believe you said that!"

"Sorry." Emma's face flushed. "I didn't mean it, Syd. It was just a joke!"

"Not funny!" Sydney snapped. "Not funny at all."

"I'm sorry," Emma repeated.

"There's been too much joking about killing each other," Sydney declared. "Way too much. Let's just stop it. Agreed, Emma?"

"Okay," Emma said. "But what are we going to do to stop Jason?"

"I don't know!" Sydney cried. "Look, I'm sick of sitting in this car. Let's go call the tow truck. We can talk on the way and figure something out."

The two girls left the car on the side of the road. Then they started hurrying down Division Street, searching for a pay phone.

The chilly spring wind ruffled Sydney's hair and carried the scent of early flowering trees. The sky turned rosy from the setting sun.

Sydney hardly noticed. All she could think about was Jason.

What can we do? she wondered frantically.

She glanced at Emma. Her friend's features were tight with fear.

No wonder she's scared, Sydney thought. She almost died. Twice.

They reached a pay phone. Sydney waited until Emma finished calling the tow truck. Then she said, "I think we should go to the police."

"And say what?" Emma asked skeptically. "Tell them your boyfriend is trying to kill us so he can have the money we stole?"

"Well, we wouldn't exactly put it like that," Sydney replied.

"How else can we put it?" Emma demanded. "There is no way we can talk to the police without the money coming out. If we didn't tell them about it, Jason would tell them. You know he would. As soon as they started questioning him."

"I guess you're right."

"I know I am." Emma slung her bag over her shoulder. "Come on. We have to walk back and meet the truck."

"Wait a second, Emma!" Sydney cried, grabbing

her arm. "This whole thing is just too much! I've been a wreck since we found that money. Please, let's go get it and turn it in, and tell the police everything!"

"Sydney, no!" Emma protested. "My mother and I need that money so much!"

"Enough to die for?" Sydney demanded.

"No, of course not," Emma replied. "But ever since we found it, all I can think about is giving it to Mom for her operation."

She shook her head. "I know I've talked about all the stuff I want to buy for myself. I know I sounded very greedy. But really, Syd, I need the money for one thing—Mom's operation."

"I know," Sydney agreed softly. She bit her lip, frustrated. She wanted to get rid of the money so badly, she'd almost forgotten about the operation.

This is like a nightmare, Sydney thought. I feel trapped in a nightmare, with no way to wake up.

"Don't tell the police about it," Emma pleaded. "Please. There has to be another way!"

"What way?" Sydney asked as the two of them walked back to the car. "If Jason really is trying to get the money for himself, what can we do?"

Emma stopped suddenly.

She clutched Sydney's arm. "Hey, I have a great idea!" she announced.

"I think it's going to solve all our problems."

chapter

13

"*T*his better not be another joke about killing people," Sydney warned.

Emma shook her head. "It's not. I promise. Here's what we do, Syd. We cut Jason in on the money!"

"You mean offer to give him some of it?"

"Not just some—a third of it," Emma said. "We make him a partner, see? Then we'll all be on the same side."

She stared hard at Sydney. "Is that a great idea or what?"

"Yes!" Sydney agreed. "It's a fantastic idea!"

Now Emma's mom will have her operation, she thought.

We'll all have some money.

And nobody will die. . . .

* * *

They returned to Emma's house. Emma insisted that Sydney call Jason and have him come over so they could tell him about their offer.

"I want him to know now, before anything else happens," she explained. "Then I'll be able to sleep tonight."

Jason drove over quickly. He climbed out of his car with a curious expression on his face. "What's up?" he asked, gazing back and forth between Sydney and Emma.

Sydney stared at him for a moment. If only I could read his mind, she thought.

Did he try to kill Emma? Did he really do that?

"What's up?" Jason repeated. "Why are you two staring at me like that?"

"Emma's brakes—they were cut," Sydney blurted out. She narrowed her eyes at Jason. "You fixed her car. But her brakes were cut. We—we almost . . ." The words caught in her throat.

Jason's mouth dropped open. "I tested the brakes!" he declared. "They worked fine. Really!"

"But, Jason—" Emma started. "You—"

"After I finished working on the car, I drove it for blocks," Jason told them. "There was nothing wrong with the brakes. Nothing. I swear!"

Sydney studied Jason's face. He's telling the truth, she decided. He's so upset. He *has* to be telling the truth.

"Are you two okay?" he asked. "Did the brakes totally go out? That's so scary."

"We were lucky," Emma replied softly.

They talked about the brake lines for a while. Jason said that sometimes in old cars the brake lines get brittle and snap.

Emma pulled Sydney aside. "I don't know whether to believe him or not," she whispered. "Now I'm totally confused. Could someone else have cut those lines? Did they just snap?"

"I believe him," Sydney replied. "Did you see how upset he got?"

"I guess we should tell him about sharing the money," Emma whispered.

Sydney nodded.

"What's the big secret?" Jason demanded impatiently. "Why all the whispering?"

"Go ahead, Sydney," Emma urged. "Tell him."

"It was your idea," Sydney said. "You tell him."

Jason groaned. "Well, *some*body tell me!"

"Okay." Emma tossed her hair back. "It's about the money Sydney and I found. We thought maybe you'd like to have some of it. Say, about thirty-three thousand dollars."

Jason's blue eyes grew wide. Then he narrowed them skeptically. "Is this a joke?"

Sydney shook her head. "No joke. We want to share it with you."

Jason stared at them a few seconds longer. Then his face broke into a wide grin.

"Man, this is unbelievable!" he cried. "Whoa!"

With a whoop, he lifted Sydney off the ground and spun her in a circle. He set her down and kissed her, then gave Emma a hug.

"Unbelievable!" Jason repeated. He did a little shuffle-dance in the driveway. "I'm too excited to stand still!" he exclaimed.

"That's how we felt when we found it," Emma told him. "You can't believe what it feels like to stare at a hundred thousand dollars."

"Hey!" Jason grinned. "Great idea! Let's do it. Let's go stare at it!"

"Now?" Sydney asked. She really didn't feel like digging up the money. Trying to think of a good excuse, she glanced around and saw clouds gathering in the sky.

"It's going to rain," she said.

"Yeah. Besides, we can't touch that money for a while," Emma added. "We have to wait and make sure nobody's looking for it."

"I don't mean we should take it out and start spending it," Jason told her. "But come on. Let me at least get a peek at it. Please?"

Emma rolled her eyes. "Well, I guess it wouldn't hurt just to *look* at it." She turned to Sydney. "What do you think?"

Sydney hesitated, then shrugged. "Okay. Let's go." After all, she thought, as long as no one sees us there, what can happen?

chapter

14

The clouds had grown thicker by the time Sydney pulled her car up to the edge of the Fear Street Woods. "Let's hurry," she urged. The three of them climbed out. "I don't want to get stuck out here in a rainstorm."

"Don't worry," Jason assured her. "We're just going to take a quick look. I don't want to get soaked, either."

He took Sydney's shovel from the trunk and hoisted it on his shoulder like a rifle. "Lead me to the treasure!" he declared.

Emma started along the path that led to the willow tree. Sydney followed, and Jason brought up the rear.

The sun had already gone down. Clouds hid the moon. Walking through the dark woods, Sydney jumped every time a twig snapped or branches rustled.

I wish we hadn't come, she thought, glancing around nervously. Why did I let Jason talk me into it?

"There it is," Emma called out, pointing toward the drooping willow tree. "Get ready to dig, Jason."

As they hurried toward the tree, a sharp, cold rain began to fall. It bounced and spattered off the leaves and began to turn the ground to mud.

Emma kicked the rock away from under the tree. Jason stuck his shovel into the ground. "You know what I'm going to buy?" he asked, tossing a load of dirt aside. "A new car."

Sydney watched as Jason shoveled up another chunk of dirt. His arms moved smoothly, and his gold school ring glittered on his hand.

"What about you, Emma?" Jason asked. "What are you going to use your share for?"

"My mother needs an operation," she told him. "After that, I'm not sure. We need lots of things."

Sydney shivered as an icy raindrop rolled underneath her collar and snaked down her back. We should have brought three shovels, she thought, rubbing her bare arms. At least the exercise would keep me warm.

The wind picked up, and Sydney shivered again. "I'm going to the car to get my sweater," she announced.

Emma glanced up. "We're almost down to the money bag," she said. "Don't you want to see it?"

"I'll see it when I come back." Rubbing her arms, Sydney took off down the path. Maybe she'd just turn on the heater and wait in the car. Being in the woods in the dark gave her the creeps. And she didn't really want to see the money, anyway.

I almost wish I'd never seen it, she thought.

Halfway along the path, Sydney heard a rustling sound. She stopped, her heart pounding.

It's nothing, she told herself. An animal, scurrying through the brush.

Giving herself a shake, she began to walk on.

And stopped—frozen in terror—as a shrill scream tore through the woods.

chapter
15

"Nooo!" The scream rang out again.

Sydney gasped.

It's Emma! she realized.

With a cry, Sydney spun around.

Ignoring her pounding heart and rubbery legs, she tore down the path.

Batting dripping branches out of her way, Sydney raced back toward the willow tree.

When it finally came into view, she stumbled to a stop. And gasped.

Emma and Jason struggled under the canopy of willow branches. They both gripped the shovel between them. Wrestling, pulling, shoving each other.

"I should have known better!" Emma cried.

"Too bad!" Jason snarled, trying to pull the shovel from Emma's grasp.

"Too bad for *you!*" Emma screamed.

She yanked on the shovel.

Jason stumbled but didn't fall.

"Give it up, Emma!" Jason's school ring gleamed in the shadows as he pulled hard again.

Emma stumbled toward him. Then she suddenly let go of the shovel.

Jason staggered backwards.

The shovel fell from his grip.

Emma dove for it.

Both of them shouted.

No words. Just shouts of hatred.

Sydney finally found her voice. "Stop it!" she shrieked. "Stop it!"

Emma scrambled up, dragging the shovel with her. As Jason turned toward the sound of Sydney's voice, Emma gripped the shovel like a baseball bat . . .

. . . And swung it as hard as she could.

The blade made a whining sound as it sliced through the air.

Sydney screamed again as the blade hit Jason in the back of the head.

The sickening *clang* echoed through the trees.

Then the only sound was the dripping rain.

Jason stood frozen for a few seconds. A raindrop rolled from his hair, down his nose, and into his open mouth.

His lips moved. He groaned softly.

Then his knees buckled.

His eyes rolled back into their sockets.

Sydney watched in horror as Jason sank to his knees. Groaned again. Then pitched face-forward onto the muddy ground.

chapter
16

*S*ydney stared at Jason across the rain-soaked path. *Get up!* her mind screamed at him. *Get up!*

Jason didn't move.

With a groan, Emma flung the shovel away. She dropped to her knees in the mud beside Jason.

Go over there! Sydney told herself. Jason might be bleeding. He needs help!

But Sydney didn't move.

Her feet felt frozen in place.

"Emma?" she called out in a hoarse whisper.

Emma slowly raised her head. Her blond hair fell in wet tangles across her face. Her frightened eyes peered between the strands.

"He's . . . he's dead!" Emma moaned.

The woods seemed to tilt and grow even darker. Sydney's stomach flipped over.

She clamped her hands over her mouth and staggered as if she'd been punched.

No! He can't be dead! she thought in a panic. Please! Please! He can't be!

She closed her eyes and took a deep, shuddering breath. Then another.

When she looked again, Jason still lay facedown in the mud.

And Emma still gazed up at her, a horrified expression locked on her face.

It's true, Sydney told herself. Jason *is* dead.

"Why were you fighting?" she choked out, still not moving from the path. "What happened?"

"He wanted all the money," Emma replied. "As soon as we uncovered the bag, he grabbed for it. He was going to take it and run, Syd! Just take the bag and run off with all our money!"

Sydney gulped in some more air.

Greedy Jason, she thought. Emma was right.

Emma was right all along.

"I tried to talk to him," Emma continued. "I told him he could have more than a third. I said he could have half. That you and I would split the other half."

"And he said no?" Sydney murmured.

"He laughed at me!" Emma declared. She pushed her hair out of her eyes, leaving a streak of mud across her forehead. "He wanted all the money! He was desperate for it."

"And then what happened?" Sydney asked. She had to ask. She had to know.

"I started to pick up the bag. And then . . . he swung the shovel at me!" Emma cried. "He almost hit me, Sydney! He would have killed me!"

Emma paused, gasping for breath.

"And then?"

Emma swallowed hard. "I grabbed hold of the shovel and . . . I guess you saw the rest."

Sydney nodded.

Her stomach churned again, and she had to swallow before she could speak. "Now we have no choice," she finally whispered.

"What do you mean?"

"We *have* to call the police," Sydney declared.

"No!" Emma jumped up and hurried over to Sydney. "We can't do that! We can't let Jason ruin both our lives!"

"But Emma, we haven't just taken a bag of money," Sydney argued. "Now . . . we're *murderers!*"

Murderers. The ghastly word echoed in her ears. *Murderers . . . murderers . . .*

"No. Only me," Emma said. "I'm the murderer. I fought with him, Sydney. I hit him. *I* killed him— not you."

"Emma, listen to me," Sydney insisted. "We have to call the—"

Emma gripped Sydney's arm. "I'll take care of everything, Syd. You won't have to do anything. Really."

71

"I don't understand!" Sydney cried. "What can you do? We can't just leave him lying here!"

"I know." Emma bit her lip and glanced around. "The lake!" she announced. "I'll sink his body in Fear Lake. He won't be found for months."

An image of Jason's body deep beneath the cold, dark waters of Fear Lake rolled through Sydney's mind.

Murderers . . . murderers . . .

She wrapped her arms around herself and shuddered violently.

"Syd, I'll take care of everything," Emma repeated, squeezing Sydney's arm. "You're practically in shock. Just stay right here, okay?"

Sydney nodded, her teeth chattering.

Emma hurried back to the willow tree. Working frantically, she filled the hole with dirt again and tossed the shovel onto the path.

Sydney couldn't stop shaking. Hugging herself tightly, she stumbled to a nearby tree and braced herself against its cold trunk.

She watched, horrified, as Emma rolled Jason onto his back and grabbed him under the arms.

Emma grunted and yanked.

Jason slid a few feet. His arms dragged in the mud and his head fell back.

Emma yanked again. Jason's feet made a thudding noise as she dragged him over tree roots.

Sydney squeezed her eyes shut. If only I could shut out the horrible sounds, she thought as she heard Emma's ragged breathing and another thump of Jason's feet.

If only I could shut out this whole night!

Bushes rustled and twigs snapped.

Sydney opened her eyes a slit and saw Emma dragging Jason into the woods. In seconds, they were out of her sight.

Murderers . . . murderers . . .

The rain had stopped. Sydney heard the drip, drip of water from the leaves. And the quiet lapping of Fear Lake as the wind blew across it.

Then she heard another sound.

A loud, sickening splash.

Emma shoved Jason in the lake, she thought with another violent shudder.

Sick to her stomach, Sydney leaned against the tree and tried to blot the horrible picture from her mind.

It's over, she kept telling herself. It's over. No one will know it was us.

She waited, tense and shaking, for Emma to return.

Emma will tell you it's over, Sydney thought. She'll tell you everything's going to be all right.

"Sydney!" Emma's voice cried out.

And Sydney knew something was wrong. Horribly wrong.

Because terror filled Emma's voice. "Help!" she cried. "Sydney—help me!"

chapter

17

"Sydney!" Emma cried again. Her voice was closer now, and Sydney could hear her ragged breathing. "Sydney! Help!"

Sydney shoved herself away from the tree and tried to move. But her head spun and her knees still shook. She fell against the tree again as Emma burst out of the woods.

"What is it?" Sydney cried. "What happened?"

Emma bent forward and grasped her knees. "He . . ." she gulped. "He won't sink!" She straightened up and flung her tangled hair back. "I need to tie something to him to make him sink."

Another wave of nausea washed over Sydney. She forced it back and leaned her forehead against the rough bark of the tree trunk. "I can't do anything," she whispered hoarsely. "This is making me sick, Emma!"

"I know. I told you I'd handle it, and I will," Emma assured her. "I just need to figure out a way to get him to sink."

Stop saying that, Sydney thought as her stomach churned and twisted. Stop talking about sinking him!

"I can tie a big rock to him," Emma said. "But I don't have any rope or anything. Can I use that?"

Sydney blinked and slowly raised her head. "What?"

"Can I use your belt?" Emma asked, pointing.

Sydney glanced down at the narrow red belt looped through her jeans. The movement of her head made her feel sicker than ever.

"Can I use it?" Emma repeated.

"Sure," Sydney muttered. She fumbled with the buckle. Anything, she thought. Anything to get this over with!

Her fingers shook wildly, but she finally managed to undo the buckle and slide the belt through the loops. "Take it," she murmured, holding it out. "I'm sorry, Emma. Sorry I'm not helping. I feel so sick I can't think!"

"It's okay," Emma told her, taking the belt. "Stay here, Syd. I'll be back real fast, and then we'll go home."

Emma raced off through the woods again. Sydney leaned back against the tree. The second she shut her eyes, the world tilted again and her stomach churned violently.

Dropping to her knees, she bent over the muddy path and vomited until her stomach muscles ached. Tears streamed from her eyes.

When it was finally over, she rose unsteadily to her feet and reached for the tree trunk. It felt damp against her forehead. Damp and cool. She leaned her burning cheek against it—and heard something.

Voices. At least two of them.

Sydney's heart began to race. Someone else is in the woods! she realized. Emma and I—we're not alone!

chapter

18

*T*he voices were too far away for Sydney to make out what they were saying.

But loud enough for her to know they were getting closer.

Get out of here! she ordered herself, her pulse racing. Get away before they see you.

She took two steps, then froze again.

Emma! She couldn't leave Emma here!

As Sydney stood in a panic, she suddenly realized the voices had vanished.

Where did they go? she wondered. They were coming this way! They couldn't just disappear like that!

A sudden rustling of leaves and branches made her jump. She spun around—and saw Emma trudging toward her through the thick woods.

"Emma! Thank goodness you're here!" Sydney cried. "Did you hear someone talking?"

"No." Emma stumbled wearily into the clearing. Mud covered her jeans. Globs of it clung to her hands and face and hair. "Nothing. I didn't hear a thing."

Sydney gazed around. Nothing moved except the branches swaying in the wind. "I was so scared and everything. My mind must be playing tricks on me."

"Maybe." Emma glanced around nervously. "But let's get out of here."

"Okay, but . . ." Sydney hesitated. "Did you . . . ? Is Jason . . . ?"

Emma nodded, her face grim. "He's gone."

Twenty minutes later, Sydney pulled her car to a stop in front of Emma's house. The dashboard clock read ten P.M.

Sydney could hardly believe it. It had been only a few hours ago that she drove over here, thinking she was going to the mall.

"I guess . . ." Sydney's throat felt raw and she swallowed. Neither she nor Emma had spoken since they left the woods. "I guess I'd better go home."

Emma still didn't speak.

Sydney gazed at her. In the dim glow of the dashboard lights, she saw tears glistening on her friend's cheeks. "Emma?" she asked. "Are you okay?"

Emma shook her head. "It's just . . ." She paused, sobbing. "I did it, Syd. I killed him!"

As Emma cried, Sydney reached out and put a hand on her shoulder.

"It's just starting to sink in," Emma sobbed. "I was numb before. That's why I could do what I did, I guess. But now it's starting to sink in."

Sydney nodded, her throat tight.

Emma turned in the car seat, her eyes filled with horror. "I killed somebody! And tomorrow we have to go to school! How can we just go back to school as if nothing happened?"

Sydney squeezed her shoulder. "Nobody at school will ever suspect us, Emma," she murmured. "Besides, we don't have any choice. The only thing we can do is act normal until they find his body."

Listen to yourself, Sydney thought. You just talked about Jason's body the way you'd talk about an old shoe or something!

"I guess you're right." Emma wiped her face again and glanced toward her house. "I'd better go in now and clean up before Mom gets home."

"Okay." Sydney sighed. "Try not to worry, Emma. Everything's going to be all right."

But how can it be? Sydney wondered as she pulled away from the little house. We took money and hid it. And now Jason is dead.

Murdered.

How can everything possibly be all right?

* * *

Sydney let herself quietly into her house. She tiptoed across the marble-floored foyer, then down a wide hall into the west wing of the house.

The sound of her parents' voices, chatting softly, drifted from the partly open door of the den.

I can't let them see me like this, Sydney thought. Even if I weren't all dirty, they'd take one look at my face and start asking a zillion questions. But she had to let them know she was here.

Quickly, she tiptoed to the staircase that led up to the bedrooms. Halfway up, she stopped.

"I'm home!" she called out, trying to sound cheerful.

"Hi, honey," her father called back. "You're a little late, aren't you?"

"I guess." Sydney tried to come up with an excuse, but her mind was blank. "Sorry."

"Anything going on at the mall?" her mother asked.

"Not much. I'm going to take a bath and study some more. See you in the morning." Before her parents decided to come out and see her, Sydney hurried up the stairs and into her bedroom.

The minute she closed the door, she began to shake again. Images and sounds flashed through her mind—the drip of rain, the rustle of leaves. The horrifying *clang* when the shovel hit Jason's head. His eyes rolling back just before he toppled into the mud.

Still shaking, Sydney hurried into her bathroom and stripped off her muddy clothes. She filled the tub with hot water, added rose-scented bath oil, and climbed in.

The bath soothed her nerves. She stayed in for a long time.

Think about other things, she instructed herself. She cleared off her bed and slipped under the covers. Think about the history test. Maybe then you'll be able to sleep.

Closing her eyes, Sydney tried to remember everything she'd learned about the Civil War and Reconstruction.

When she woke up, the first thing she saw was her bedside clock. Three-thirty in the morning.

With a sigh, she rolled onto her back.

Someone stood at the foot of her bed.

"Mom?" Sydney asked, her voice groggy with sleep. "That you?"

No answer.

The figure moved slightly. As it did, a shaft of moonlight fell across its face.

Jason!

It can't be! she thought. It can't be!

But it was. Jason stood at the foot of her bed, gazing at her.

Mud and pond scum covered his shirt.

Strings of slimy algae hung from his hair and wrapped around his neck.

Dark blood caked the back of his head and his shoulders.

"You—you're dead!" Sydney gasped.

But as he stared down at her, his eyes were filled with life.

And with blame.

chapter
19

"**N**o!" Sydney screamed again. "You're dead! You're dead!"

With a terrified sob, she flung out her hand to turn on her bedside light.

Her hand hit the shade. The lamp wobbled and began to fall.

"No!" Sydney scrambled off the bed. Grabbed the lamp before it crashed to the floor.

Gasping, Sydney switched it on.

Backing against the wall, she held the lamp high. "Jason—?"

No one there.

No one.

"Sydney?" her father called from the hall. He knocked softly on the door. "I heard you yell. Are you all right?"

"I . . . I'm fine," Sydney called back in a trembling voice. "I had a bad dream."

It seemed so real, she told herself. But it was only a nightmare.

"Sydney, are you sure you're all right?" her father asked.

No, Sydney thought. Not yet. Maybe not ever.

"Sure," she answered. "Sorry I woke you, Dad. Good night."

" 'Night, honey."

Sydney rose to her feet, her heart still pounding. Her hands shook as she set the lamp back on the table.

Emma, she thought. I wish I could call her. Tell her what I saw.

Glancing at the clock, Sydney realized it was way too late to be making phone calls.

Besides, it *was* only a nightmare.

It had to be.

Jason was dead, deep beneath the surface of Fear Lake.

As she climbed into bed again, leaving the light on, Sydney wondered if Emma was having nightmares, too.

A buzzing sound filled Sydney's ears. A constant, annoying drone.

Without opening her eyes, she flung her arm out and punched the snooze button on her alarm clock.

I'm so tired, she thought, snuggling her head deep into the pillow. So tired.

And then she sat up straight, suddenly remembering all that had happened.

Jason!

Emma killed Jason last night. He died under the willow tree. She tied a rock to him and sank him in Fear Lake. And then I had that awful nightmare.

Slowly, Sydney gazed at the foot of her bed.

Jason had stood right there, she thought. Bleeding and covered with mud. Staring down at me. Blaming me.

His eyes filled with such hate.

Sunlight poured in through the windows, warming the bedroom. But Sydney felt herself shivering. She drew the thick comforter around her shoulders and wrapped her arms around her knees.

Jason is dead, she told herself. He's really dead.

Still shivering, she leaned her head on her knees and took a shaky breath. Was she going to dream about him every night?

Another buzz rang in her ears. Sydney jumped, then shut the alarm off. If she didn't get moving, she'd be late for school. It was the last place she wanted to go. But she knew she had to act normal.

Pretend everything was fine. Pretend she hadn't watched Jason die. Hadn't seen him lying face-down in the mud under the willow tree.

Stop it! Sydney told herself. Don't think about it anymore!

Throwing off the bedcover, she hurried into her bathroom to get ready. The clothes she'd worn yesterday still lay in a muddy heap on the tile floor. With a shudder, she stuffed them into the hamper.

After a fast shower, Sydney wrapped herself in a thick, white robe. She stood in front of the mirror. Her eyes had dark circles under them. Her hand shook as she combed out her wet hair. The bathroom was steamy, but she still shivered.

You're totally messed up, but you have to go to school, she kept telling herself. You have to act as if everything is normal.

The comb tangled in her hair. She slammed the comb down and hurried out of the bathroom.

In her walk-in closet, Sydney studied the long rows of clothes and tried to decide what to wear. Jeans? A skirt? Something colorful? Or something black?

What do you wear the day after you helped kill your boyfriend?

Stop it! she ordered herself again. Just pick something and go to school.

Sydney grabbed jeans and a cinnamon-colored blouse. As she started to the bed, she stopped.

No! she thought. No!

Her ears rang and her pulse raced. Shaking her head, she took two more steps.

And stared at the carpet at the foot of her bed.

Deep in the ivory carpet, she saw two footprints.

Two muddy footprints.

Jason's footprints.

chapter

20

"It had to be a dream, Sydney."
Emma slammed her locker and snapped the lock.

Sydney tensely twisted a strand of hair around her pointer finger.

"But what about the footprints, Emma?" she asked, her voice rising. "They didn't vanish the way Jason did. They were there this morning, oozing mud into the carpet!"

"Ssh!" Emma hissed, nudging Sydney's arm. "You want somebody to hear you?"

Sydney glanced around the hall. Kids were hurrying to the first class of the day.

"Of course not," she whispered. "But those footprints really freaked me out, Emma. I didn't dream those footprints. They were definitely real!"

"Okay. They were," Emma agreed. "And I just realized how they got there."

"How?"

"It's easy to explain. We were both out in the muddy woods, right?" Emma pointed out. "So . . . the footprints were *yours!*"

Sydney stared at her. "You think?"

"Of course!" Emma insisted. "I was totally covered in mud and gunk when I got home last night. My clothes were a disaster and so were my shoes. Weren't yours?"

Sydney nodded slowly.

"Plus, you were totally freaked," Emma reminded her softly. "You weren't paying any attention to where you walked or stood. You just wanted to get out of those wet, filthy clothes, right?"

"Right. I was practically hysterical," Sydney admitted. "I don't remember much, except that I took a bath." She took a shaky breath. "I guess you're right. They *could* be my footprints."

"They *are* yours," Emma corrected her. "I know it was an awful dream, Syd. But come on—we both know dreams don't leave footprints."

Emma has to be right, Sydney thought, as she watched her friend hurry to her first class. She has to be right . . .

"Hey, Sydney." Tori Johnson smiled as they walked out of English together. "Where's Jason?"

"He . . ." Sydney's heart raced. She felt her face grow hot. "I'm not sure."

Tori raised her eyebrows skeptically. "You two are always together. How could you not know where he is?"

She stared at Sydney as if searching for the answer in her eyes. Then she gasped. "Don't tell me you broke up with Jason!"

No. I just helped kill him, Sydney thought.

The image of Jason standing at her bed flashed through her mind again. She shook it away and forced a smile.

"No, we didn't break up," she said. "I just haven't seen him today, that's all. He must be out sick."

Tori nodded and sped off down the hall.

Sydney sighed and went in the other direction, toward her locker.

Tori wasn't the only one who'd asked her about Jason today. It seemed as if the entire school wanted to know where he was and why they weren't together.

And every time someone asked, Sydney's heartbeat speeded up and she blushed. She was such a terrible liar. It was a miracle that anyone believed a word she said.

Someone tapped her shoulder. Startled, Sydney whirled around.

Kurt Walters, a guy from her history class, stood grinning at her. "Sorry. Did I scare you?"

"A little." Laughing nervously, Sydney began walking again.

Kurt fell into step with her. "That history test was really tough, huh? How do you think you did?"

"Probably flunked it," Sydney muttered.

At least *that* wasn't a lie. Everything she knew about the Civil War had vanished from her mind.

"Yeah, well, join the club," Kurt told her. "Hey, where's Jason?"

Not again! Sydney thought. Why did I ever come here today? I should have known people would wonder why Jason and I aren't together.

Kurt stared at her. "So, is he around?"

"No." Sydney bit her lip and glanced away, wondering if Kurt could hear her heart jackhammering in her chest. "I haven't seen him. Have you?"

"If I had, I wouldn't be asking *you*."

"Oh. Right." Sydney forced a laugh. "I think he must be sick."

"Yeah. I guess." Kurt gave her another curious glance, then shrugged. "Well, see you."

"Sure." He knew I was lying, Sydney thought as Kurt walked away. He could tell!

Sydney sighed. She was the one who told Emma they had to act normal today. But she had practically jumped out of her skin the first time anyone asked her about Jason.

At least the day is over, she thought as she approached her locker. She could go home. Take another long bath.

And try to forget about Jason.

As Sydney opened her locker, something slipped

from the shelf and fell to the floor. She glanced down.

At her feet lay a small envelope, folded in half.

Huh? She hadn't put any envelope in there. Maybe it was a flyer for a bake sale or something.

Curious, Sydney bent down and picked it up.

Her fingers touched something moist.

Mud. A smear of damp mud covered the front of the envelope.

Sydney shivered, remembering the muddy footprints on her carpet.

Get a grip, she told herself. It rained again this morning. Everything is muddy.

Sydney turned the envelope over. Something heavy slid to one corner.

She ran her fingers over the bulge. Definitely not a flyer.

Quickly, she ripped open the envelope and peered inside. Something gold glinted up at her.

Her hands shook as she slid it into her palm and stared at it.

A ring. A Shadyside High school ring, with the owner's initials carved into it.

J. P.

Jason Phillips.

Jason's ring, Sydney realized.

I saw it on his hand last night.

chapter

21

A dull roar filled Sydney's ears.

Her vision blurred. The hallway started to spin.

Her hand shook so badly, she had to squeeze her fingers around the ring to keep from dropping it.

Jason wore this ring last night! her mind screamed. I saw it on his finger. I saw it gleaming when he was shoveling under the tree!

How did it get here?

Sydney slowly uncurled her fingers.

Jason's ring gleamed in the palm of her hand.

"No," she whispered, shaking her head violently. "No!"

"Sydney, what's wrong?"

Startled, Sydney turned quickly, banging her shoulder on the sharp edge of her locker door.

Emma stared at her, a concerned expression on her face.

"Emma," Sydney whispered in a hoarse voice. "You're not going to believe this."

"Believe what?" Emma asked, frowning. "What is the matter with you, Syd? I saw you shaking your head and mumbling to yourself."

"Look!" Sydney opened her fingers and held out the ring. "It's Jason's school ring."

Emma's eyes bulged.

"I found it in my locker, inside that envelope." Sydney pointed to the muddy envelope that had fallen to the floor. "See the mud? It's still damp."

"Syd . . ."

"How did Jason's ring get in my locker?" Sydney demanded shrilly. "He was wearing it when he . . . last night! I saw it, Emma! I saw it on his hand, I know I did. So how did it get here?"

"Sydney, calm down and let me think!" Emma replied impatiently. "I don't remember seeing it last night, Syd. Are you sure he was wearing it?"

"Yes, I'm sure. Well . . . almost."

"Well, maybe you just thought you saw it," Emma suggested. "Anyway, Jason could have left it here yesterday. He used your locker before, right?"

"Right, but . . ."

"And the gym is just down the hall," Emma continued. "So maybe he put it in here before gym class. You know, so he wouldn't lose it."

"But, Emma, I went to my locker two times

today," Sydney argued. "And the envelope wasn't there!"

"Are you sure?"

Sydney closed her eyes and tried to remember. She had gone to her locker that morning, hung up her jacket, taken out some notebooks. Then after lunch, she had put away the morning notebooks and taken out the ones she needed for afternoon classes.

"Well?" Emma asked.

"I'm pretty sure it wasn't there," Sydney told her. She sighed. "But—but—I'm not sure of anything anymore!"

"Then I bet the ring was in your locker all this time," Emma declared. "It was probably stuck in a book or something."

"Do you think so?"

"Come on. It had to be there!" Emma insisted. "There's no other explanation."

Sydney stared at her, still shaken. "First the muddy footprints," she murmured. "Now this. I thought . . ."

"Stop thinking about it." Emma squeezed her arm. "You're freaking, Sydney. You have to get a grip!"

"I'm trying!" Sydney cried. "But everybody keeps asking me about . . ." She glanced around and lowered her voice. ". . . About Jason. Where is he? Why isn't he with me? It's driving me crazy! And now I find his school ring in my locker!"

"I know. But it must have been there already and

you just missed it." Emma squeezed Sydney's arm again. "That's what happened, Syd. Please don't fall apart!"

Sydney forced herself to breathe deeply. Emma was probably right about the ring, she thought. And she was definitely right about falling apart.

You have to get a grip, Sydney ordered herself. You have to!

Sydney stuffed Jason's ring into the pocket of her jeans. Then she raked her fingers through her hair and managed a smile. "I'm better now," she murmured. "I'll be okay."

"Good." Emma smiled back. "Come on. Let's get out of here. Today was the worst. It will get easier after this."

I hope so, Sydney thought. I can't take many more days like this.

Sydney grabbed her jacket. "Do you want me to drop you off at the Cineplex?" she asked as they walked down the hall.

"No. But you can give me a ride home," Emma told her.

"Aren't you working?"

"I called and said my head is still bothering me." Emma touched it and winced. "It was no lie, either. It's pounding right this very minute. I'm going to lie down as soon as I get home."

Me, too, Sydney thought, pushing open the doors that led to the student parking lot. I'll take a hot bath, and then I'll take a nap.

I just hope I don't dream about Jason.

Clouds covered the sky outside, but the rain had let up. Skirting the puddles, Sydney and Emma hurried through the parking lot to the car.

Emma pulled open the door and began to toss her backpack inside. "Oh, no!" she gasped.

"What? What's wrong?" Sidney cried.

Emma's face had gone pale. Her finger shook as she pointed. "Look!"

Sydney stared into her car.

And felt a cold wave of fear ripple up her spine.

A shovel lay on the seat, caked with mud.

But not just mud, Sydney realized.

Splotches of blood.

Dark red blood, still shiny and wet, smeared the shovel and dripped onto the pale beige seat cushion of her car.

chapter
22

Sydney stared at Emma in disbelief. "But—but—how did it get here?" she sputtered. "What is that thing doing in my car?"

"I don't know!" Emma wailed. "I—I didn't put it there last night!"

"What do you mean?" Sydney demanded. "What did you do with it last night? Didn't you hide it?"

"Let me think!"

Emma squeezed her eyes shut. "After I hit Jason, I tossed the shovel down," she said slowly. "I—I forgot all about it. I never went back and picked it up."

"So how did it get into my car?" Sydney demanded.

"I'm telling you, I don't know!" Emma cried.

She glanced back at the shovel, then gasped. "Sydney, someone must have seen us!"

Another ripple of fear shot up Sydney's spine.

"You heard voices, right?" Emma asked. "When I came back from burying Jason in the lake, you told me you heard people talking, remember?"

"I remember." Sydney clenched her jaw to keep her teeth from chattering.

"I thought you were just freaked," Emma continued. "But I was wrong. You were right, Syd. Someone else *must* have been in the woods."

Someone watching us, Sydney thought with a shudder. Hiding and watching.

"Whoever it was found the shovel, Syd!" Emma cried. "And they put it in your car to threaten us!"

"Threaten us? Why?" Sydney whispered hoarsely. "I mean, do you think they saw what happened with Jason? Or did they just find the shovel after they saw us running away? Why did they put it in my car? What do they want?" She couldn't keep the panic from raising her voice high and shrill.

"We'll have to wait and find out, I guess," Emma replied with a shudder. "I'm scared, Syd."

Me, too, Sydney thought. But I'm not just scared. I'm *terrified.* She glanced into the car again.

The shovel still lay there, smearing mud and blood onto the seat cushion.

With a cry, she grabbed the shovel, dragged it out of the car, and shut it in the trunk.

"What should we do now?" she asked breathlessly, climbing into the driver's seat.

"I'm not sure," Emma replied. She wiped the mud off her seat and got into the car. "But we're both too scared to think right now. We might do something dumb. Let's go to your house and try to calm down. Then we can talk about what to do."

"Okay." Sydney's hand shook badly as she jabbed the key at the ignition.

She finally got it in on the third try, and the engine roared to life.

As she peeled out of the parking lot, she hit a speed bump so hard that her head banged the car roof.

"Slow down!" Emma warned. "The last thing you want right now is a speeding ticket!"

She's right, Sydney knew. If I got stopped now, I'd totally fall apart.

Easing up on the gas, she glanced at Emma. "Should we take the shovel and hide it someplace?" she asked. "Should we bury it, maybe? Or wash all the blood off and then take it back to my house?"

Emma shook her head. "Someone might be watching us, remember?"

Sydney's stomach flipped over. Her heart pounding, she raised her eyes to the rearview mirror.

That blue car trailing behind her—had it been there all along?

Keeping her eyes on the mirror, Sydney drove north on Park Drive.

The blue car stayed with her.

Sweat broke out on her forehead. She gripped the wheel and forced herself not to push the gas pedal to the floor.

One block.

Two blocks.

The blue car stuck with her.

Sydney turned into the North Hills section of Shadyside.

The blue car followed.

Who is it? she wondered. Someone who saw us in the woods? "Emma?" she finally murmured. "Check out the blue car behind us."

Emma quickly turned in her seat. "What blue car?"

Sydney glanced in the mirror.

Behind her stretched an empty road.

"It *was* there!" Sydney insisted.

"I believe you," Emma told her. "Did it tailgate you or something?"

"No. I just thought it was following us. I—I guess I'm feeling totally paranoid." Breathing a sigh of relief, Sydney drove carefully through North Hills.

Ten minutes later, she pulled her car into the garage. She and Emma entered her house.

Her parents weren't home, thank goodness.

The day's mail lay on the foyer table. It had been separated into three piles—Sydney's, her mother's, and her father's.

Sydney grabbed her pile, then led Emma into the kitchen and took two cans of soda from the refrigerator. "Come on. Let's go to my room before anybody else gets home. The last thing I want to do is answer questions about how my day was and how I did on the history test!"

In her bedroom, Sydney tossed down her backpack and mail. The mail scattered across the rug. A magazine. A bill for the insurance on her car. And a plain white envelope with no return address.

Curious, she picked up the envelope. She put her soda can on the night table, then sat on the bed and ripped open the envelope.

Inside was a single sheet of white paper, folded in half.

As Sydney unfolded it and read the typewritten words, a wave of dizziness washed over her.

"What's wrong?" Emma asked. "Your face just got totally white."

Still dizzy, Sydney licked her lips and clutched the letter tightly.

"Syd? What's wrong?" Emma repeated. "What does it say?"

Sydney cleared her throat. "I saw you in the woods," she read in a trembling voice. "I know your name. It's *Murderer.*"

chapter

23

Sydney heard a whirring in her ears, as if she were in a wind tunnel. Letting the note fall from her hands, she gazed across the room at Emma.

Emma stared back, her blue eyes wide and frightened.

For a moment, neither of them spoke.

Finally, Sydney whispered, "This isn't a nightmare. And I'm not being paranoid. This is really happening!"

Emma snatched up the note and read it herself.

Sydney drew her legs onto the bed and wrapped her arms around her knees.

"What are we going to do?" she cried hoarsely. "Somebody knows what happened, Emma! Someone knows that we murdered Jason!"

Emma raked her fingers through her long blond hair. "No one can prove we killed him," she declared. "I mean, Jason hasn't even been found yet. And when he is found, we have each other as alibis."

"But, Emma," Sydney cried. "If somebody *was* watching, then they must know where you put Jason's body!"

Emma didn't respond, but her face turned pale. She crumpled the note and tossed it into the wastepaper basket.

Sydney couldn't sit still. She slid off the bed and began to pace the room, twisting a strand of hair around her finger as she walked back and forth.

"Sydney, sit down, will you?" Emma pleaded. "You're making me even more nervous!"

"I can't help it." Sydney paced some more, then stopped suddenly. "My belt!" she gasped, spinning around to face Emma.

"Huh? What about it?"

"You used it to tie that rock around Jason. Emma, we have to go back and get my belt before anyone finds it!"

"No way!" Emma cried. "We're not going back to the lake. I'm telling you, Syd, whoever sent that note doesn't know what really happened. They're bluffing!"

"What makes you so sure?" Sydney demanded.

"I . . . well . . ." Emma finally shook her head. "I guess I can't be positive," she admitted.

"So we have to go back!" Sydney repeated. "We have to get my belt. And we have to hide the body someplace else!"

Half an hour later, Sydney followed Emma through the thick tangle of weeds and bushes toward Fear Lake.

I've never been so scared in my life, she thought. Scared of moving Jason. Of touching his dead body.

Scared of getting caught.

Something brushed across Sydney's face. She jumped back with a cry.

Emma glanced over her shoulder. "Just a tree branch, Syd. Come on. We're almost there."

Sydney forced herself to keep going. I can't believe I'm doing this, she thought. I can't believe I got myself into this mess because of some stupid money!

Up ahead, Emma climbed over a fallen log, then disappeared through some thick undergrowth.

Sydney hurried to catch up. She jumped over the log, then scrambled through the tangle of bushes, emerging at Emma's side.

Ten feet ahead of them stood Fear Lake.

A breeze blew across the water, making small waves that lapped against the shoreline.

It was late afternoon. Clouds filled the sky, and the water of Fear Lake lapped softly, dark and cold.

Sydney gazed out at it, her heart pounding.

"Are you sure this is the right place?" she whispered.

Emma nodded. "I remember that log back there. I had to drag Jason's body around it. Didn't you see how the weeds were flattened?"

"No." Sydney shuddered and hugged herself. "I wasn't exactly paying attention."

"Okay. Let's get it over with." Emma took a deep breath, then stepped to the edge of the lake.

Sydney followed, her knees feeling like jelly. "How far out did you take him?" she asked.

"Not far," Emma replied. "There's a drop-off a little way out. You feel like you're stepping off a cliff. But it's really only a few feet down to a sort of underwater ledge. I rolled him down onto it. Come on."

Leaving their shoes and socks on the shore, they rolled up their jeans and waded into the icy water.

Sydney shuddered again as strings of algae wrapped themselves around her ankles.

Is Jason covered with algae? she wondered.

Have the fish discovered him? Will he be bloated and bitten, like bodies in the movies?

Don't think about it, she told herself. You'll go crazy if you think about it.

She wiped the slimy scum off and trudged forward.

When the water reached almost to her knees, Emma stopped wading. "This is it," she told Sydney.

She pointed to an old wooden shed not far from where they stood. "I remember looking at that pier when I was out here. We're in the exact same spot now."

"Okay. Let's do it."

Sydney shoved her sleeves up, then plunged her hands into the water. Her fingers grasped pond scum, soft and slimy.

She stuck her arms down farther. Rocks. Sand. More pond scum.

No Jason.

She raised her eyes to Emma. "Did you find him?"

"Not yet."

Emma's long hair spread out across the water as she bent over, plunging her arms in deeper. After a moment, she straightened up. Her hair dripped and her hands held nothing but algae.

"He should be right here!" she cried. "This is where I put him."

Sydney waded in deeper, until the water reached halfway up her thighs. We have to get my belt back before his body is found! she thought.

"He couldn't be any farther out!" Emma gasped as she struggled through water up to her waist. "There's no tide or anything."

"I know. We'll find him," Sydney declared, her teeth chattering. "We have to find him!"

The sky grew darker. Sydney's feet felt like blocks of ice. Her hands and arms turned numb.

"I don't get it," Emma sighed. "I just don't understand why we can't find him!"

Sydney's whole body shook with cold. She stared out at the murky waters. It's useless to keep looking, she realized.

Jason is not here.

His body is gone!

chapter

24

"Someone moved him," Emma declared as Sydney drove them away from Fear Lake. "That's the only explanation."

Sydney turned the heater on and gripped the steering wheel tightly.

Emma is right, she thought. Somebody found Jason's body and took it out of the lake.

But who? And why?

"It can't be the police," Emma said, as if she'd read Sydney's mind.

"Why not?"

"Because the police would have told his parents. And everyone would know that Jason is dead. And they'd be asking questions all over the place," Emma replied. "You know. Who saw him last?

Who was with him? They would have come looking for us already."

Sydney turned the heater up higher. Hot air blasted out, but she still couldn't stop shaking.

"Then it had to be whoever saw us that night," she murmured through clenched teeth.

"Yeah." Slumped in the passenger seat, Emma held her hands in front of the heating vent. "Do you think someone is after the money?" she asked.

"Nobody knows it's there but us," Sydney reminded her. "Whoever was in the woods didn't see it."

"Maybe Jason told somebody about it," Emma suggested. "You told Jason, remember? And he could have told someone else. I bet he did," she added with a bitter laugh. "I bet he bragged his big mouth off about it to somebody! What do you think, Syd?"

"I don't know," Sydney replied softly. "I don't have any idea what's going on!"

The only thing I know for sure, she thought, is that everything has gone wrong.

Horribly wrong.

After dropping Emma off at her house, Sydney drove home in a daze. As soon as she pulled around to the garage, her heart sank.

Both of her parents' cars were home.

I can't face Mom and Dad now, she thought. I just can't. No way can I come up with an excuse for being totally soaked and covered with lake slime!

Easing her car into the garage, Sydney cut the motor and climbed out.

She left the garage door open, so that the noise wouldn't alert her parents. Then she walked behind the garage, around the pool, and over to the west wing of the house.

Standing in the damp grass, she gazed up at the wooden deck jutting out from her bedroom.

Stairs led up to the deck, and sliding glass doors opened into her room.

Please don't let the doors be locked! she pleaded silently.

Carrying her shoes, Sydney quickly tiptoed up the steps and onto the deck.

A phone rang inside the house.

Sydney's heart raced as she heard footsteps.

Then her mother's voice carried through an open window.

She's talking to my grandmother, Sydney realized. They'll be on the phone for at least half an hour. And Dad is probably playing computer chess by himself, as he usually does before dinner.

Sydney trotted across the deck and carefully pulled on the sliding door.

It slid open soundlessly on its track. Sighing with relief, Sydney stepped into her bedroom.

Without even turning on a light, she hurried into her bathroom and took the hottest shower she could stand.

Finally warm, she dried off and slipped into her thick, white bathrobe.

110

As she came out of the bathroom, someone rapped lightly on her door.

"Sydney?" her mother called. "Are you in there?"

"Yes, I just got out of the shower." Sydney started for the door, then stopped.

She wasn't soaked anymore. But she knew her face would show that something was wrong. "I came in by my deck because my shoes were all muddy."

"Fine. Your father and I are going to a fund-raising dinner in about an hour," her mother said. "You'll have to make some dinner for yourself."

"Okay." Sydney felt a wave of nausea at the thought of food.

"How did the test go?"

Sydney's mind went blank. What test?

"I'm sure you did great," her mother called in. "History is your best subject."

Right. History.

"It was pretty hard," Sydney told her. "Anyway, Mom, I'm tired. I think I'll just hang out for a while."

"All right. I'll let you know when we leave."

Thank goodness her mother wasn't the type to barge in, Sydney thought. But she knew she couldn't hole up in her room forever.

Don't worry about that now, she told herself. You have enough to worry about.

Sydney rushed to the bed and turned on the lamp.

Soft light spilled out over the thick green comforter and the stuffed animals piled on top of the pillows.

Sydney reached for Goldy—a fat brown teddy bear she'd had since she was three.

As Sydney lifted the bear from the bed, something else came with it.

Something long and red, tied around Goldy's leg.

Sydney gasped as she stared at it.

My belt! she realized.

My red belt!

The belt Emma used to tie the rock to Jason.

Who put it here? Who tied it around Goldy's leg and put it in my room?

With a cry, Sydney ripped the belt off. As she did, something white fluttered down and landed on the bed.

Another piece of white paper, folded in half.

Sydney's mouth went dry. Her heart began to hammer.

She picked up the paper and unfolded it.

Inside was a one-word message: MURDERER.

But this message had been written by hand.

Sydney's pulse thundered in her ears as she stared at it.

She recognized the handwriting.

She knew who wrote this note.

Jason.

chapter
25

A scream of horror rose in Sydney's throat. She swayed on her feet.

The note slipped from her hand and dropped to the bed. It landed next to the red belt.

Sydney sank onto the bed, sick and terrified. As she collapsed against the pillows, her hand flew out and hit the telephone.

Emma! she thought, bolting up again. I have to tell her!

She grasped the phone and dragged it off the table. The numbers blurred in front of her eyes.

Finally, she managed to punch in Emma's number.

"Hello?" Emma's voice sounded wary.

"Emma, it's me!" Sydney cried, her voice trembling.

"Syd, I'm really glad you . . ."

"Emma, I know what's happening!" Sydney interrupted. "I know who sent me the note and put the ring in my locker! I—"

"Syd, slow down!" Emma urged. "You're going too fast. I can't understand you."

Sydney choked back a sob. She forced herself to take a deep breath. Finally, she was able to talk again.

"Remember my red belt?" she asked. "The one you used to tie the rock to Jason?"

"Yes. Of course."

"It's *here,* in my room!" Sydney cried. "I found it just now. Somebody tied it around Goldy's leg."

"Whose leg?"

"Goldy, my old . . . Oh, what difference does it make? The belt is here!" Sydney cried. "And there was a note, too. It said 'Murderer.'"

Emma gasped.

"Somebody put the belt and the note in my room—and I know who it was!" Sydney announced.

"Who?" Emma demanded anxiously.

"Jason."

Emma gasped again. "Whoa! Sydney . . ."

"Listen to me!" Sydney jumped up and began pacing back and forth by the bed. "The note is in Jason's handwriting, Emma! I'd know it anywhere!"

Emma remained silent.

"Don't you get it?" Sydney continued. "It's not

somebody who saw us out in the woods. It's Jason himself."

Her voice rose. "He was dead, right? Emma? You were sure he was dead?"

"Yes. He was dead," Emma replied in a whisper.

Sydney was silent for a moment. "Do you believe in ghosts?" she asked in a tiny voice. "I don't know—"

"Syd, I was just about to call you," Emma broke in. "I got a note, too. With the same word on it—'murderer.'"

"You see?" Sydney cried. "It's him. It's Jason! Who else could it be?"

"Somebody from school," Emma replied. "Someone Jason talked to. That's what I thought the second I saw the note."

"What about the handwriting?"

"Someone copied it," Emma declared. "Now listen, Syd. We have to figure this out. Someone wants to scare us—really bad. We can't get hysterical. We have to think."

"I can't!" Sydney cried, her voice rising even higher. "I can hardly breathe! I almost fainted when I saw the note, Emma! I'm so scared, and I don't know what to do!"

"I'm coming right over," Emma said. "I'll borrow my neighbor's car. Hang in there!"

After Emma hung up, Sydney held onto the phone until it beeped, startling her. She hung it up and began pacing the room again.

Every time she turned, she saw the red belt and

the small sheet of white paper lying on the bed next to Goldy.

I have to get out of here! she thought. I can't stand being in this room.

Still in her bathrobe, Sydney pulled open the sliding door, ran down the deck steps and around the house to the garage to wait for Emma.

Hurry, Emma! she thought, pacing barefoot up and down the rough cobblestones. I can't keep it together much longer. I'm going to start shrieking my head off any second!

At last, headlights rounded the corner of the house. A dark brown station wagon pulled to a stop. Emma climbed out. Sydney ran over and threw her arms around her friend.

"Thank goodness you're here!" she cried, hugging Emma tightly. "I'm so scared!"

"Ssh," Emma murmured. She held her by the arms. "Syd, what are you doing out here like this? Your hair's all wet and you're barefoot."

"Waiting. I couldn't wait inside," Sydney told her. "I took a shower. That's why my hair is wet. Then I got out of the shower, and that's when I found . . . the belt and . . ." She broke off.

Emma squeezed her arms. "Syd, please. Try to hold on."

"I'm trying," Sydney gasped. "But I'm so scared. Aren't you? First Jason's school ring. And now the belt—how did the belt get here?"

She shuddered.

"Do you believe in ghosts, Emma? I never did. But now—"

Emma took hold of Sydney's arms again. "You've got to keep it together, Sydney," she declared. Her blue eyes were filled with worry. "You're really losing it. You look terrible. And you're not making any sense."

"I can't help it!"

"You have to!" Emma gave Sydney a little shake, then put an arm around her shoulders. "Let's go to your room, okay? Show me the belt and the note."

Sydney took a deep breath and nodded. "Okay. But we have to go in through my deck. I don't want to run into my parents."

"Definitely not," Emma agreed. She took Sydney's arm and walked her up the deck steps.

Emma pushed the sliding door all the way open. Then she tugged gently on Sydney's sleeve. "Come on, Syd. Show me the belt."

Sydney stepped hesitantly through the door. Her eyes snapped immediately to the bed.

"Oh no! I don't believe it!" she cried.

chapter
26

"They're gone!"

Sydney rushed to the bed. "The belt. The note. They're both gone, Emma!"

"You—you left them on the bed?" Emma stammered.

Sydney nodded. She scanned the carpet.

Empty.

She ran around to the other side of the bed, dropped to her knees, and searched underneath.

No note. No belt.

"They were right here!" Sydney insisted, pounding her fists on the mattress. "Emma—they were right here ten minutes ago."

Emma strode to the bed and picked up the teddy bear.

"That's Goldy," Sydney told her. "The belt was

tied around his leg. See the mud? Some of it came off on his fur. Do you see it?"

Emma checked out the bear's legs and arms. Then she turned to Sydney. "I don't see any mud on him."

Sydney snatched the bear from Emma's hands and carefully inspected each leg.

No mud.

She tossed the bear across the room. It landed with a soft plop next to the door.

"This is impossible," she gasped. "I know what I saw. They couldn't have just disappeared."

Frantic to find the note and belt, Sydney scooped up the rest of the stuffed animals and threw them on the floor. She shoved the pillows off and pulled the comforter down.

"Sydney, stop," Emma told her. "They wouldn't be under the covers."

"They have to be." Sydney wadded the comforter into a big ball and tossed it aside. "They have to be here someplace."

She yanked the sheets off and stared at the bare mattress, panting in fear and frustration.

"Sydney, there's nothing there!" Emma cried.

"Okay. So they're not on the bed."

Wading through the mound of stuffed animals, Sydney crossed the room to her closet. She pulled open the closet door and stepped inside.

"Sydney, come on!" Emma cried. "They're not in the closet!"

"Right!" Sydney backed out. Her head felt about

119

to explode. "They couldn't hop off the bed and hang themselves up, could they?"

She scowled as she glanced around the room. "But they were here before. So they have to be here now."

As Sydney strode back to the bed, Emma grabbed her arm. "Sydney, forget it!"

"What do you mean?"

"The belt and the note aren't here," Emma declared. "Forget looking for them."

"But they *were* here," Sydney insisted. "You think I made them up?"

"No, but . . ." Emma paused.

"But what?" Sydney pulled her arm away. "You think I'm crazy?"

"Of course not! But Syd, you're not thinking clearly," Emma replied. "You're not sleeping or eating, and you have nightmares. And look around. Look what you did to your room just now."

Sydney gazed around the room. Stuffed animals scattered all over the place. Sheets dragged to the floor, the comforter spilling off the chair.

"It's a wreck," Emma said softly. "And if I didn't stop you, you'd turn the whole house upside down looking for that belt and the note."

"They were here," Sydney whispered. "They were here."

"You've got to get a grip, Syd. Please." Emma squeezed her arm. "I need you. I need your help. I think you should go to sleep. Everything will seem better in the morning. I know it will."

"I would love to sleep," Sydney sighed. "But I'm afraid I'll have a nightmare."

"I don't think you will," Emma told her. "You're exhausted. You'll probably sleep for twelve hours and not have a single dream."

A dreamless sleep, Sydney thought. That would be wonderful.

Emma picked up the tangled sheets. "I'll help you make the bed, okay?"

Sydney nodded, then jumped as someone tapped on the door.

"Sydney, are you on the phone?" her mother called. "I heard voices."

"I don't want her to see me!" Sydney whispered. "She'll know something's wrong."

"It's me, Mrs. Shue," Emma called back quickly. "Emma. I stopped by to drop off some English notes. Sydney is in the bathroom."

"Okay. Bye, Emma. Tell Sydney we're leaving."

As her mother's footsteps faded away, Sydney took a shuddering breath. She stood in the middle of the room, while Emma remade the bed.

"There." Emma plopped a handful of stuffed animals on top of the pillows and smiled. "Ready to go to sleep?"

Sydney gazed at the bed, thinking about the red belt. "Syd?"

"I'll walk you downstairs," Sydney told her. "I want to get a Coke or something."

"But you'll come back up and go to sleep, right? You promise?" Emma insisted.

"Sure."

Downstairs, in the marble-floored foyer, Emma gave Sydney a hug. "I'm so worried about you, Syd."

Sydney forced a smile. "I'll be okay. Really."

"Have hot chocolate instead of soda," Emma suggested. "It will help you sleep."

"Right."

Sydney pulled open the door and watched as Emma strode away. In a few moments, the station wagon's headlights swept around the side of the house. The station wagon pulled down the long driveway and out of sight.

Sydney stood there for another minute, then shut the door and started back upstairs.

She didn't want hot chocolate.

She didn't want to sleep, either.

She wanted to find that belt and that note.

They were there, she told herself. I saw them. I'll find them.

Won't I?

Upstairs, she threw open her bedroom door and flipped on the light switch.

And screamed.

Jason hunched in front of the sliding deck door, staring at her with dead, sunken eyes.

chapter

27

Sydney stood frozen, her hand still on the light switch.

Her heart seemed to stop.

She squeezed her eyes shut, willing the horrible figure to disappear.

But when she opened her eyes, Jason still stood across the room.

Mud and pond scum covered his clothes. Dark red blood matted his hair and formed a dried, crusty smear on his shoulders.

The skin on his hands and face had turned greenish-black.

Like moldy bread, Sydney thought.

He's rotting! she realized. I can smell him from here. He's dead and rotting!

Jason's lips quivered. A piece of rotting flesh slid

from his bottom lip and slithered to the floor. His teeth were cracked and covered with green slime.

"*Sydney,*" Jason rasped. His voice sounded hollow, as if from far away.

Dead.

He *is* dead! Sydney thought in horror.

I'm not dreaming.

I'm not imagining it.

Jason has come back from the dead!

"*Sydney,*" Jason rasped again.

Sydney almost choked from the stench of his rotting skin. She wanted to cover her nose. But her hand slipped from the light switch and fell limply to her side.

Jason stared at her, his eyes sunk deep in his skull.

And then he took a lurching step toward her.

Something was tied around one of his legs. Something long and muddy.

And red.

My belt, Sydney realized.

The end of the belt flapped as Jason lurched forward. Sydney wanted to run. But her legs wouldn't cooperate. She had to lean against the wall to keep from falling.

Jason took another step. "*You killed me,*" he choked out.

No! Sydney wanted to scream. But she couldn't move. She couldn't even shake her head.

"*Emma killed me, and you watched,*" Jason's

124

hollow voice accused. *"Emma murdered me. And you helped her."*

Whimpering in terror, Sydney slid down the wall to the rug. Her hand touched something soft and furry.

Goldy.

With another whimper, she dragged the teddy bear onto her lap.

Jason came closer.

The rotting stench grew stronger.

The air turned cold.

"Emma killed me," Jason whispered. *"You killed me."*

Sydney fell onto her side. She drew her legs up to her chest.

"You killed me . . . you killed me . . ."

Clutching the bear in both hands, Sydney curled herself into a tight ball.

Jason drew closer.

Sydney whimpered.

She smelled his rotting flesh. She heard his dead, empty voice. *"You killed me . . ."* he repeated. *"You killed me."*

And then Jason's shadow rolled over her.

And she felt the cold.

The cold of death.

chapter

28

Emma tapped her foot and glanced nervously around the hospital waiting room.

In spite of the colorful pictures on the walls and the cheerful yellow chairs, the place gave her the creeps. She hated hospitals.

Deal with it, she told herself. You have to be here. You have to find out if everything is going to be all right.

Magazines had been fanned out across every tabletop in the room. Emma took one and flipped through it, then slapped it back on the table.

She felt too edgy to read.

She glanced at the big wall clock. Only two minutes had passed since she checked it last.

With a nervous sigh, she stood up and paced

back and forth in the small waiting room, forcing herself not to check the time again.

An elevator bell pinged somewhere down the hall.

Two nurses strode by, talking softly.

What's taking so long? Emma wondered. Why isn't there any word yet?

Go get another soda, she told herself. You'll kill at least five minutes that way.

As Emma rummaged in her bag for some change, the door across the hall whooshed open.

Emma jumped to her feet and rushed into the hall, her heart pounding.

A white-coated doctor stood in the doorway, turning his head to talk to someone behind him.

"I thought she was ready to see you," the doctor said. "But she can't let go of this idea that you're dead. I'm sorry."

The doctor emerged from the doorway.

Jason followed him.

The door whooshed shut behind them.

The doctor put his hand on Jason's shoulder. "I'm sorry," he repeated gravely.

"I understand," Jason murmured. "I just hate to see her this way. We used to be so close." He took a deep breath and gazed at the floor. "And now she thinks I'm some kind of monster."

Giving Jason's shoulder a sympathetic squeeze, the doctor nodded at Emma, then strode away.

Jason stared at the floor a moment longer, then

he raised his sad blue eyes to Emma. "Let's get out of this place."

Silently, the two of them left the hospital and walked out to the parking lot together.

Jason unlocked his car and they climbed inside.

Emma swept her long hair back and turned to Jason. "Well?" she demanded.

Jason grinned at her, with no trace of sorrow in his eyes. "You were right. Sydney is completely nuts!"

Emma breathed a sigh of relief. "I knew it would work. I knew she would crack if she thought you had come back from the dead to haunt her."

"Yeah. She just holds on to that teddy bear and twists her hair around her fingers like a baby," Jason said.

"She always did that when she was nervous," Emma told him. "She never could handle pressure."

"And now she is *gone*, man. Totally flipped," Jason declared. "She'll be in that hospital forever."

Emma smiled in satisfaction. "I told you we could get rid of her this way."

Jason started the car and revved the engine.

As they peeled out of the parking lot, Emma glanced back at the red brick hospital building.

She knew Sydney's parents would take her out of there soon. They'd put her in some private place, with gardens and ponds and rooms as big as Emma's house. And then Sydney would go home.

But her parents would never believe her story.

It will cost them a fortune, Emma thought. But so what? They can afford it.

That was why Emma had gone to Jason as soon as she and Sydney found the bag of money.

Sydney didn't need it. She was already rich.

Right from the start, Emma worried that Sydney wouldn't keep their secret. Sooner or later, Sydney's conscience would get the better of her.

Sydney would start to feel guiltier and guiltier.

She'd tell her parents about the money. Or she'd tell the police.

Emma couldn't allow that.

Emma really needed that money. And she knew that Jason needed it, too.

She and Jason had been sneaking out together for weeks. They pretended not to like each other. They didn't want Sydney to catch on.

Now, they had the money—and they had each other.

Emma glanced over at Jason. She chuckled to herself. When she'd told him her plan to drive Sydney nuts, Jason leaped at the chance to help.

"What's so funny?" Jason asked.

"I was just thinking how easy it was to fake your death," Emma told him. "Sydney was so stupid that night at the lake. She never even checked to see if you were breathing or not. She just took my word for it."

"Lucky us," Jason murmured.

129

"Yeah, that was the trickiest part," Emma agreed. "After that, I knew everything would be great."

She shook her head. "Later, when I was supposed to be dumping you in the water, she heard us talking. And she thought someone else was in the woods. She didn't have a clue." Emma laughed again. "It was so easy . . . so easy."

"Enough yakking about it," Jason told her. "It's over, right? We're safe and in the clear. So let's go dig up the money."

"What a good idea!" Emma exclaimed. "Then— straight to the mall. I'm really going to celebrate! For the first time in my whole life, I really can shop till I drop!"

Emma stood in front of the three-way mirror at Hidebound, an expensive leather shop. She gazed at her reflection.

The leather jacket felt buttery-soft, and it fit her perfectly. It made her look rich, too.

You *are* rich, she reminded herself with a grin.

She and Jason had raced to the woods and dug up the money bag. Wow. What a thrill!

She brushed dirt off the bag and practically tore it open. She'd grabbed two stacks of fifties. Stuffed one stack in her jeans pocket. Tossed the other stack to Jason.

Then they heaved the bag into the trunk of his car—and took off on their shopping spree.

Now she grinned at her reflection in the leather jacket. She glanced at the price tag dangling from the sleeve.

Six hundred dollars.

No big deal.

"Are you about done?" Jason asked impatiently.

Emma turned to him. "I'm trying to decide whether to get this in black or brown."

She spun around, showing off the black jacket. "What do you think?"

Jason shrugged. "That one looks awesome. Hurry up, will you? I want to go next door and check out the wide-screen televisions."

"Okay, okay." Emma walked over to a cashier. She eased out of the jacket and draped it across the counter. "I'd like to take this," she said.

The salesman, a young, red-haired man in a leather sports coat, glanced at the price tag. "A very good choice," he said. "This is Italian leather. One of our best buys."

He raised his eyes to Emma. "How would you like to pay for this?" he asked.

"I'll pay cash," Emma told him.

She felt so excited. Her whole body tingled. So this was what it felt like to be rich!

She pulled the stack of fifty-dollar bills from her pocket and counted out six hundred dollars. Then she handed the money to the cashier.

He took the bills and began shuffling through them, counting.

Then he stopped—and laughed.

"Wh-what's so funny?" Emma demanded.

"These are really good!" the clerk said, still snickering.

"Huh? Good?" Emma cried.

The clerk handed the bills back to her. She and Jason held them close and examined them.

It took Emma a few seconds to see what the clerk was talking about. She was totally confused until she read the words across the top of the bill: UNTIED STATES OF AMERICA.

And then her eyes lowered to the engraved portrait of Benjamin Franklin.

His eyes were crossed and he wore a backwards baseball cap over his wig.

Emma grabbed the counter to keep herself from falling. Slowly, she raised her gaze to the red-haired salesclerk.

"Did you bring any *real* money?" he asked.

About the Author

R.L. Stine invented the teen horror genre with Fear Street, the bestselling teen horror series of all time. He also changed the face of children's publishing with the mega-successful Goosebumps series, which *Guinness World Records* cites as the Best-Selling Children's Books ever, and went on to become a worldwide multimedia phenomenon. The first two books in his new series Mostly Ghostly, *Who Let the Ghosts Out?* and *Have You Met My Ghoulfriend?* are *New York Times* bestsellers. He's thrilled to be writing for teens again in the brand-new Fear Street Nights books.

R.L. Stine has received numerous awards of recognition, including several Nickelodeon Kids' Choice Awards and Disney Adventures Kids' Choice Awards, and he has been selected by kids as one of their favorite authors in the National Education Association Read Across America. He lives in New York City with his wife, Jane, and their dog, Nadine.

DEAR READERS,

WELCOME TO FEAR STREET—WHERE YOUR WORST NIGHTMARES LIVE! IT'S A TERRIFYING PLACE FOR SHADYSIDE HIGH STUDENTS—AND FOR YOU!

DID YOU KNOW THAT THE SUN NEVER SHINES ON THE OLD MANSIONS OF FEAR STREET? NO BIRDS CHIRP IN THE FEAR STREET WOODS. AND AT NIGHT, EERIE MOANS AND HOWLS RING THROUGH THE TANGLED TREES.

I'VE WRITTEN NEARLY A HUNDRED FEAR STREET NOVELS, AND I AM THRILLED THAT MILLIONS OF READERS HAVE ENJOYED ALL THE FRIGHTS AND CHILLS IN THE BOOKS. WHEREVER I GO, KIDS ASK ME WHEN I'M GOING TO WRITE A NEW FEAR STREET TRILOGY.

WELL, NOW I HAVE SOME EXCITING NEWS. I HAVE WRITTEN A BRAND-NEW FEAR STREET TRILOGY. THE THREE NEW BOOKS ARE CALLED FEAR STREET NIGHTS. THE SAGA OF SIMON AND ANGELICA FEAR AND THE UNSPEAKABLE EVIL THEY CAST OVER THE TEENAGERS OF SHADYSIDE WILL CONTINUE IN THESE NEW BOOKS. YES, SIMON AND ANGELICA FEAR ARE BACK TO BRING TERROR TO THE TEENS OF SHADYSIDE.

FEAR STREET NIGHTS IS AVAILABLE NOW. . . . DON'T MISS IT. I'M VERY EXCITED TO RETURN TO FEAR STREET—AND I HOPE YOU WILL BE THERE WITH ME FOR ALL THE GOOD, SCARY FUN!

RL Stine

I felt cold, hard bony fingers tighten around my neck. I fell to the ground, twisting and thrashing, trying to squirm away, trying to fight it off. But my whole body was heavy with panic. And I couldn't breathe . . . couldn't breathe. . . .

Beside me, I saw Jamie—eyes wide, mouth locked in a wide O of horror—being strangled . . . strangled by the skeleton, a hideous grin on the dirt-caked skull.

The strong, bony hands tightened around my throat and squeezed.

Twisting to pull free, I felt something drop onto my back. And then something hit my shoulders. I saw dirt flying . . . dirt falling into the hole. Falling on my head, my back. . . .

I couldn't breathe . . . couldn't breathe at all.

The dirt fell into the hole from above.

And over the roar, I heard that ghostly woman's voice: *"You'll pay . . . you'll ALL pay now . . ."*

The mountain of dirt was flying, flying and falling, filling up the hole again.

The two skulls grinned. The hard, bony hands tightened and squeezed.

And the dirt rained down.

My last thought: Jamie and I . . . no one will find us.

No one will ever know where we are.

We are being strangled—and buried alive!

Feel the fear.

FEAR STREET® NIGHTS

A brand-new Fear Street trilogy by the master of horror

R.L. STINE

In Stores Now

Simon Pulse
Published by Simon & Schuster
Fear Street is a registered trademark of Parachute Press, Inc.

the party room

by Morgan Burke

The party room is where all the prep school kids drink up and hook up. All you need is a fake ID and your best Juicy Couture to get in.

One night, Samantha Byrne leaves with some guy no one's ever seen before . . . and ends up dead in Central Park. Murdered gruesomely. Found at the scene of the crime: a school tie from Talcott Prep.

New York is suddenly in the grip of a raging media frenzy. And a serial killer walks amidst Manhattan's most privileged—and indulged—teens.

From Simon Pulse
Published by Simon & Schuster